Kiss Me, Katie

Monica Tillery

CRIMSON
ROMANCE
F+W Media, Inc.

This edition published by
Crimson Romance
an imprint of F+W Media, Inc.
10151 Carver Road, Suite 200
Blue Ash, Ohio 45242
www.crimsonromance.com

SBN 10: 1-4405-6858-8
ISBN 13: 978-1-4405-6858-9
eISBN 10: 1-4405-6859-6
eISBN 13: 978-1-4405-6859-6

Cover art © 123rf.com

Acknowledgments

I'd like to thank my wonderful friends who read and critiqued the earliest versions of *Kiss Me, Katie*. Your endless support and enthusiasm for this project are what kept me going, and without you I never would have come this far. I certainly would have given up long ago, and I am forever grateful for your steadfast belief in me.

Thank you to Matt Thompson, world traveler, drummer extraordinaire, and real-life professional rock star, for advising me. Your input helped lend authenticity to Blake and Katie's story, and you saved me from making some major mistakes. You are awesome!

Finally, and most importantly, I have to thank my fantastic husband, Dave, for believing in me and encouraging me to write when there was no guarantee that success would come. To be loved and supported in such a way is an incredible gift. That's good stuff.

Chapter One

With just hours to go before her band Sterling took the stage to open for country music megastar Blake Jackson, Katie McCoy was supposed to be in her dressing room waiting for the road crew to set up equipment for sound check. She couldn't resist a little sneak peek at the arena before it filled up with Blake Jackson's adoring fans, so she wandered around the stands, her pink cowboy boots clicking on the smooth concrete floor. She viewed the stage from all angles, imagining what it would feel like to play in front of such a huge crowd. Crew members swarmed around the stage, running wires and cables, setting up chairs, props, and platforms, testing equipment.

Katie clasped her hands in front of her chest and sighed with delight as the band's giant banner was unfurled at center stage. Sterling's logo was fresh and bold on the crisp new banner. It had cost the band a fortune, but the euphoria of seeing it hanging above the stage convinced Katie that it was money well spent. She could almost hear the crowd cheering, could feel the hot stage lights warming her skin, and she let herself slip into a daydream. Her band would play flawlessly, the crowd would go wild, and then she'd take her bows in front of the roaring fans, who would of course be begging for an encore. She smiled and giggled to herself, hoping that the reality would be even half as good as the dream.

"Hey, doors don't open until seven." A deep and tantalizingly familiar voice came from the stands above her. Katie froze, her heart pounding, and spun on her heel at the sound of the voice. Katie knew she wasn't alone in the arena, but she didn't realize that anyone had noticed her. She would've kept the giggling and excitement confined to her dressing room had she known there was an audience. She looked up and was shocked to see Blake Jackson sitting in the stands, a sly smile on his rugged face and worn cowboy boots propped up on a seat in front of him. Blake was America's biggest country star, happened to be incredibly handsome, and had given her band an incredible break by inviting them to open for twelve of the stops on his Country Summer Nights tour. She stood, frozen for a moment, before she registered the fact that her favorite singer was sitting just a few dozen feet away from her.

"You're Blake Jackson!" Katie stammered. *God, I sound like an idiot!* She blushed furiously and covered her face with her hands. The shock of seeing him right before her eyes when she had previously only seen him in magazines and on television stopped her in her tracks. Katie knew all of Blake's songs by heart; she sang along when they came on the radio and could play her fiddle along with the album when she was at home. He couldn't be more than five years older than her, but he had been a success in the business for much longer. There weren't many people who didn't know Blake's music.

"Yes, ma'am. Just Blake will do fine though, Miss...?" Blake's lazy Southern drawl was so appealing that Katie wasn't sure she'd be able to string together a complete sentence. She doubted that it was possible to be more flustered.

"McCoy. Katie McCoy. It's so nice to meet you, Mr. Jackson, I mean Blake; I'm a huge fan of yours. I guess I'm not really supposed to be wandering around out here, but my band is opening for you tonight and it's my first show in a place so big. It's kind of overwhelming."

"Well, Katie McCoy, let me show you around." Blake made his way down the stairs to where she waited, a bemused smile playing on his lips. Katie was sure that if he got close enough he'd be able to hear her heart pounding. She took in the lean but muscular body evident under his worn blue jeans and fitted black T-shirt and felt her breath hitch when their eyes met. His dark blue eyes sparkled with amusement under the brim of his Stetson.

"Wow," she breathed. "I mean, hi." Katie straightened her posture and swallowed the lump in her throat as Blake reached her. So the country's biggest star was standing a mere foot away from her, and he was gorgeous and smelled amazing, so what? Fainting wouldn't make the best first impression.

Blake offered Katie his arm and patted her hand when she took it. "Let's take a walk," he said.

Katie did her best to act natural as she walked beside Blake, not entirely sure her knees wouldn't buckle underneath her. His muscles rippled under her grasp as the pair made their way around the venue, wandering through the backstage area, and back around to the front of the arena. Katie was all wide-eyed wonderment, but Blake seemed completely at ease, in his element.

Blake Jackson was clearly a man who was comfortable in his own skin. He pointed out spots in the venue that Katie was sure she should try to remember for later, but his close presence was too distracting. It was all Katie could do to tear her eyes away from him as he showed her around. Walking alongside Blake, Katie found that she enjoyed the faint scent of old popcorn and stale beer in the air, and the sights and sounds of the employees and road crew at work thrilled her. This was the kind of moment that she would remember for the rest of her life, long after this tour ended.

"So you're in Sterling, huh? I've heard your single; it's called 'Valentine', right? Unless you have a very deep singing voice, I know you're not the singer. What do you play?" Blake looked down at Katie while they wandered through the concession area, ignoring the stares of the curious arena staff members. A pretty brunette dropped a stack of cups over the counter when they strolled by.

Katie smiled sympathetically at her obvious embarrassment, but Blake didn't even notice the flustered girl or the cups tumbling all over the floor. Surely he was aware of the effect he had on women but was obviously too kind to show it.

"Fiddle. I've been playing since I was a kid; in fact I've been playing your songs for years. This whole thing is just amazing. I mean, really, I can't believe I get paid to do something I love so much."

"Yeah, it sure is a fun way to pay the bills," Blake said with a chuckle.

"Well we only recently started making enough money to count for anything. Almost everything we had went into joining this tour, so for now I guess we're playing for free again. Not that I mind," Katie added quickly. "This is an amazing opportunity for us, and hopefully it will lead to bigger and better things."

"Oh yeah, I remember how long I played for bar tabs and gas money before I made enough to quit my paying jobs. And I had some dirty, sweaty jobs. I wouldn't trade that time for anything, though. Everybody nowadays just wants to be famous and nobody really puts in the time any more. If you ask me, success is a lot more satisfying when you've waited and worked for it," Blake said.

"I imagine that's so and I really hope we find out. Of course, being able to join your tour has felt like a pretty sweet success. It's actually a dream come true." Katie admitted.

"Y'all obviously deserve it, Katie. The label doesn't exactly do artists any favors. No amount of money could persuade them to put you on with me if they didn't think you could handle it. Y'all paid for your spot on this tour and you should enjoy every minute of it," Blake said.

They continued their walk through the venue, arm in arm, and Katie caught whiffs of Blake's spicy cologne and felt his body heat when she got close. Her hometown of Orange Blossom, Texas, was small but there was no shortage of good-looking guys. Being young, pretty, and in a popular band meant that Katie could take her pick of guys, but she gave most of her time and effort to music. Dating had never been a priority since so much of her time had to go to writing songs, rehearsing, and gigs with her band. Something was different about Blake, though. She had never met anyone like him. Katie couldn't remember ever being so enchanted by mere proximity to a man before, and the effect was almost disorienting.

Walking around the venue with Blake Jackson felt like something from a dream. His charisma drew Katie in, intoxicating her with his irresistible mix of confidence, charm, and approachability. It was hard to believe that the sweet man taking such an interest in her was one of the country's biggest stars. He was so open, so easy to talk to, and he really listened when Katie talked. Their walk was over too soon for Katie as the pair stopped in front of her dressing room.

"Well Miss McCoy, this is where we part ways. I better head on back and start getting ready for tonight's show. I'll try to catch your set. Hope you stick around for mine," Blake said as he smiled and tipped his hat. Katie thanked him for the tour and let herself into her dressing room.

Katie leaned against the closed door, breathed in the cool air of her empty dressing room, and waited for her pulse to slow to a normal rate. She took a deep breath and let it out slowly, forcing herself to relax. With her band's show coming up, she needed to try to forget about the delicious Blake Jackson and focus on tonight's performance.

It would take a Texas-sized effort to tear her mind away from those soulful dark blue eyes, the stubble on his gorgeous face, that touchable wavy brown hair, those soft but strong muscles… whoa. *He's just a man. A fellow human being. Who just happens to be gorgeous, talented, and sweet.*

Katie gave herself a little shake and tried to clear her mind. She looked around the dressing room at all the special touches that were there just for her. The band had been able to include riders in their contracts specifying what they required for their dressing rooms. It had been a heady experience being able to simply state what she wanted to be in place and have it all ready for her upon arrival. A sweet arrangement of daisies in a glass vase sat on her vanity, a plush pink couch was by her wardrobe, and a plastic bucket of ice contained bottles of water and iced tea. Everything was just as she had requested and even better than she had imagined. *I could get used to this,* she thought.

There was a knock on her door, and Katie's pulse raced. *Blake?* She opened the door and quickly hid her disappointment when she saw the hair stylist, armed with tools and products, ready to transform Katie from small-town girl into country music beauty. Back home in Orange Blossom, Texas, Katie was content with her girl-next-door good looks and rarely needed to dress up. She tried to look nice for gigs, but the places Sterling usually played weren't exactly fancy. Jeans, a cute top, and a little makeup were all she really needed. Being on tour with a national act was a whole different ball game, though. Playing in arenas, opening for Blake Jackson, it was so different from playing in the small clubs that they were used to. Katie had precious little experience with hairstyles, makeup, and fancy clothes and was grateful for the professional assistance.

"Hey there, I'm Katie. Come on in," Katie said as she stepped aside. She hopped into the chair in front of her huge mirror and let the stylist work her magic. Her mind drifted as the stylist chattered away and curled, combed, teased, and sprayed Katie's honey-blonde hair. The makeup artist arrived, and Katie was able to relax and sink into her daydreams while the two ladies chatted with each other over her head. She allowed herself to drift into fantasies of meeting up with Blake again, walking with Blake again, touching Blake again, maybe kissing Blake, maybe happily ever after with Blake. She smiled to herself. *This is going to be a fun gig.*

• • •

Blake sank down on to the sofa in his dressing room and kicked off his boots, letting them fall to the floor. After spending the past two months on the road with their last opening act, he was ready for something fresh, and Katie McCoy would do quite nicely. Blake had heard a few Sterling songs, but he had never seen pictures or read any interviews. He hadn't realized that their fiddler was female…and beautiful. Being single, famous, and ruggedly handsome made finding female companionship fairly easy for Blake, but spending months at a time on the road meant that every woman he met was either a fan, a reporter, or a crew member. Every fan who managed to make her way backstage had started to look and seem the same as the last, and none of them sparked his interest. Sure, they were pretty, but Blake was finding it more difficult to be content with just a pretty face and was ready for someone with more substance, something special. The women he met were certainly interested in meeting him, and they were probably nice enough, but Blake always got the feeling that none of them cared to know him as a person. Everybody wanted a piece of Blake Jackson, the country star; none of the women cared much about Blake Jackson, the man. Nobody was interested in finding out more about him than what they read in magazines or saw online. Meeting him was nothing more than an experience for the women, a photo they could show off to their friends later. The more his career flourished, the harder it was to meet a woman who didn't already know everything she wanted to know about him. Blake decided that he couldn't feel too sorry for himself, though. He was, after all, living the dream of most red-blooded American men. He picked up his cell phone and called his assistant.

After a few moments, Caroline Mathers entered Blake's dressing room with her usual cool efficiency, impeccably dressed and armed with her BlackBerry and a neat stack of papers. "Blake,

I have your schedule for today, a few interview requests we need to decide on, and a couple of choices for local staff. Did you need something special or are you ready to get down to business?" She smiled at Blake indulgently as she set the papers down on his table and patted her perfectly coiffed auburn hair.

"Caro, I'm all yours, darlin'. Whatcha got for me?" Blake crossed the room to join her and willed himself to focus on business details. It would be good for him to get his mind off the young Miss McCoy and back on the business at hand.

Blake struggled to pay attention and make clear-headed decisions as Caroline went through the day's business. The business he really wanted to focus on was Katie McCoy. He thought of her silky blonde hair and wondered what it would feel like in his hands. He remembered her surprisingly hearty laugh and was pleased to have been able to coax it from her. His mind wandered to her beautiful green eyes and he realized that he couldn't remember the last time he had actually noticed the color of a girl's eyes, much less found himself thinking that they looked like sparkling emeralds. There was something special about Katie, and Blake was willing to use his tour to explore it.

"Hey Caro, why don't we do a little meet and greet with the opener?" Blake tried to sound casual as he put his hands behind his head and leaned back in his chair.

"Ah, sure, I suppose we can set something up. You want to do drinks after the show?" Caroline remained professional and didn't question his unusual request. Blake rarely went out of his way to socialize with opening bands, staff, or press. He was friendly and welcoming to fans, and while he could be very casual with her, he was always clear that theirs was a working relationship.

"That sounds good. Would you mind finding somewhere good around here and setting it up?"

"Sure, I'll call around and see what I can do. I'm sure we can find a place that won't mind reserving a space for a large group if it includes you. We just need to make sure security won't be an issue. Let's see, they've got five guys." Caroline scanned her papers. "Wait. Make that four guys, one young lady, plus security. I guess I can figure that out when I get info on the bar itself." Understanding dawned in Caroline's eyes and a knowing smile danced across her lips.

Blake was fairly sure that Caroline could figure out what he was up to, but he continued to play it cool. Caroline had worked for him for almost five years, and since they had known each other, Blake's relationships rarely lasted more than a couple of weeks. She had to know that if he was going to this much trouble to put himself in Katie's path that it was important.

"I'll get it set up. Just let me know if you have any special requests." Caroline straightened her paperwork in her arms and moved towards the door. "I'll be on site and available all afternoon if you need me. Otherwise, I'll see you tonight after your set. Have a good show, Blake." She shifted the paperwork to one arm and let herself out.

Blake allowed himself a satisfied smile. Katie might not realize that tonight's get together would be orchestrated strictly for her benefit, but the boys in the band certainly would. He would take their good-natured ribbing, though. He had a feeling that it would be worth it.

Chapter Two

Katie couldn't tear her eyes away from the beauty queen staring back at her in the dressing room mirror. In a little over an hour, the hair and makeup team had transformed her from small-town cutie to sexy ingénue. Her wavy hair had been curled, teased and sprayed until it was a shiny mound of smooth honey-blonde curls, her eyelashes went on for miles, her lips were painted in a shimmery pink fancier than anything she'd ever applied herself, and her clothes...*wow*. She had traded jeans and a T-shirt for sequined shorts that showed off her legs and a fitted shimmery top in the most gorgeous shade of blush pink that she had ever seen. She hardly recognized herself.

"Wow, you guys...I can't believe that it's me. I have never looked like this, and I couldn't have done it myself. I feel like a princess. Thank you so much!" Katie was bubbling over with enthusiasm for the team. A brisk knock on the door interrupted them.

"Hey Katie, wait...whoa!" Her band mate, Jeff, poked his head in. He stepped in and took in Katie's new appearance. "You look beautiful."

Katie dipped her head and looked at her friend through a fringe of impossibly long dark lashes. "Aw, thanks. These girls have outdone themselves." She gestured at the hair and makeup team.

"I'll say. Anyway, we are ready for the pre-show meeting if you're good to go. Also, Blake Jackson invited us to go out for drinks tonight after his set. His assistant is going to set it up and get us the details."

"Oh, really? Well, that sounds like fun." Katie kept her excitement to herself, but the butterflies in her stomach were going crazy. She suppressed her gleeful grin as well as she could as she hopped off her chair and trailed behind Jeff to meet up with the band, waving good-bye to the girls as they packed up their tools and products. It was all she could do to keep herself from skipping.

Her arrival was met with wolf whistles and exaggerated compliments from the boys in the band. Sterling had spent so much time together between rehearsals, playing gigs, and traveling, that the guys were like big brothers to Katie. As an only child, the fierce protective nature of the guys had taken a bit of getting used to. Their attention was suffocating at times, but was often just what she needed as they traveled to some of their shadier gigs. Katie couldn't recall a time when she had ever been in actual danger, but some of the clubs and bars that Sterling played were on the scary side. It was always reassuring to know that she had four men ready and willing to protect her should she need it. Tonight she took in their appreciative looks and allowed herself to forget the stress and tension of travel and preparation and just give in to the excitement that had been building in her heart all day. This was it, the day they'd all been waiting for.

Katie forced herself to pay attention to the information and last-minute details being given to her amid the frenzy of activity before the band took the stage. They had rehearsed, their road crew had checked and double-checked everything, but this was the biggest show of their career and it seemed like what they didn't know could fill a book. Now it was time to shake off the lingering anxiety and focus on the music. There was no room for insecurity out on the stage, no hiding from the hundreds of eyes watching and ears listening. Tonight's show was a huge step for her career, not to mention the culmination of countless hours of writing music, practicing, and networking. Sterling had paid thousands of dollars to join the tour, and they needed to start earning it back.

The band members joined hands, and Jeff offered a little prayer for the group. Katie paused, offered her own silent prayer, and centered herself before heading up the stairs to the stage. As she reached the top of the steps, she could see nothing but the stage and the blazing lights illuminating it. The crowd was an undulating blur in front of them. She could hear the audience cheering and knew that anything less than their best performance would disappoint the restless fans. Blake Jackson drew the crowds, but the members of Sterling hoped to find a few new admirers of their own. Katie and her band mates emerged onto the stage under the hot lights to a roar of cheers and applause as the announcer shouted, "Please welcome, all the way from Orange Blossom, Texas, Sterling!"

All her anxiety and doubts were erased and thoughts of everything but the music, the crowd, and the energy fell away as the band played their set. Katie allowed herself to be swept away with the music, on the wave of emotion coming from her band mates and the crowd. Sterling had been playing together for six years, so the beautiful feeling of being completely in sync with each other was nothing new to Katie. She had never experienced such a surge of adrenaline during a performance, though. The sheer size of the audience catapulted the experience to a whole new level. She marveled at her hands' ability to seemingly play her fiddle on their own, and an irrepressible smile beamed on her face. *This is it,* she thought. *This is what it's all about.*

Their set lasted over an hour, but before she knew it, the band was taking their bows and heading off the stage. One of the things Katie loved most about music was its ability to take her away, to carry her to a place where hours felt like minutes. The ecstatic buzz in her head gradually gave way to the reality of the arena. The crowd was roaring, and Katie followed her band mates as if in a dream, turning to wave at the crowd one last time, a huge smile on her face.

The sea of bodies and the thunderous applause was unbelievable, and Katie threw kisses to the crowd until she was out of their sight. The euphoric buzz of pulling off such a successful show distracted her enough that she didn't notice a very special fan watching from backstage.

•••

Blake had watched Sterling's set from the side of the stage, and he was impressed. For such a relatively new band, their stage presence, technical talent, and songwriting were phenomenal. Sterling was a great addition to his tour, and it was a shame that they would only be opening for twelve shows. He thought that they could make a good team and wondered about the possibility of hiring them for more dates. The tour had been planned out months in advance, but bands dropped out for various reasons all the time. There was always a chance a spot would open up for Sterling.

Blake was sure he was biased, but Katie McCoy was one hell of a fiddle player. *She's probably a pretty good kisser, too.* Blake laughed to himself and shook his head, mentally clearing thoughts of Katie and her kissable lips, and headed to join his band for their own pre-show meeting. Blake Jackson was at the height of his career, and he could credit a single-minded determinedness for his success. When other men his age were out meeting women and dating, Blake was writing music and rehearsing. When other guys were getting engaged, Blake was making albums. Instead of building a family, he had built a career. He had never really had a serious girlfriend or given much thought to when he would marry and have children, he just focused on the music and becoming a giant in the industry. He didn't get to be one of the best in the business by distracting himself with romance and beautiful blonde-haired, green eyed fiddlers. *There would be plenty of time for that later.*

Chet Wilson, Blake's longtime fiddler, approached him with a playful glint in his eyes. "I saw you watching the opening act, boss. They put on a great show, and I noticed that their fiddler's not half bad. Pretty cute, too."

"Yep, they've got some real talent. You better keep your performance up, Chet. I might decide that I'm tired of looking at your ugly mug on stage every night. You may have competition." Blake laughed good-naturedly and clapped Chet on the back. "You ready to do this?"

"Brother, I was born ready," Chet said with a chuckle.

"All right, everyone." Blake motioned for the band members to join him in a circle. "Let's join hands." The men joined hands and the guitar player offered a group prayer. "Guys, let's get out there and show them how it's done!" Blake clapped his hands a few times, and the band bounded up the stairs onto the stage, welcomed by the screaming fans.

• • •

Katie and her band seated themselves at a secluded table together in the corner of the dark club where Caroline Mathers had sent them. Classic country music blared from a jukebox in the corner, and couples swirled around a wooden dance floor, two-stepping the night away. A couple of waitresses arrived at the band's table with pitchers of beer and glasses for everyone.

The band was still riding high on the success of their show and were congratulating each other and chatting when Blake Jackson and his band arrived. A hush fell over their celebration, and Blake walked over to their table, a smile on his face and his eyes trained on Katie. Conversations all around the bar faltered as people noticed and recognized Blake. Katie saw people whispering to one another and pointing as he walked through the bar. He stopped at their table and looked pointedly at the empty table beside the one the band was crowded around.

"Hey guys, I invited y'all out so we could all get to know each other better, so let's spread out a little. Whaddya say?" Blake gave Katie a warm smile, and his eyes lingered on hers as he started pushing the empty table over towards theirs. Katie's band mates changed seats, leaving a few empty chairs between each other, and the musicians from Blake's band filtered in and seated themselves.

Katie held her breath, hoping that Blake would take the empty seat next to her. A thrill skipped down her spine as their gazes locked and he pulled back the chair next to her. "Miss McCoy," Blake said with a nod as he sat down beside her. He treated her to a heart-melting smile as his eyes twinkled with interest.

"Mr. Jackson," she said as she lowered her eyes and looked at Blake shyly.

"So you two met already?" Sterling's singer, Charles, said with a confused look. Katie could hear the familiar protectiveness creep into Charles's question. Charles was a good twenty years older than Katie and had always had a soft spot for her. Sometimes he treated her more like a daughter than a band mate.

"We met this afternoon when Blake showed me around after we first got to the venue. We just kind of bumped into one another," Katie replied. Her heart racing, she took a sip of her beer, determined to disguise her self-consciousness.

"Oh, well, all right, then. I'm Charles, Mr. Jackson. We are so glad to be on this tour, sir. Thank you for having us," Charles said as he extended his hand across the table to Blake.

"Good to meet you, Charles, and just Blake is fine. Mr. Jackson is my father. I'm glad to have you on board." Blake shook Charles's hand. "You deserve your spot, man. You guys made this happen with no help from me."

"I guess we're just lucky then," Katie said with a nervous laugh.

"I think I might be the lucky one," Blake said under his breath. Katie thought she heard him but couldn't be sure. She chanced a shy glance up at him through lowered lashes and was equally thrilled and embarrassed when their eyes met. She forced herself to look away and attempt to show an interest in the conversation beginning around the table.

As the night wore on, the two bands shared stories and the beer flowed. They got to know each other and congratulated each other on two great shows. Blake's knee gently bumped Katie's, his hand brushed against hers in passing, and he caught her eye more than once while their band mates talked all around them.

Katie wondered if Blake was initiating any of the contact on purpose or if she was just wishing he was. She had read countless interviews and articles about Blake over the years, but she could not remember ever having read about a special woman in his life. Surely he could take his pick—women must be lining up at his door every night. Katie was surprised to feel jealousy bubbling up under the surface of her composure when she imagined his female fans coming backstage. She pictured gorgeous, scantily-clad women catching Blake's eye, maybe spending a few private hours with him, and had to deliberately calm herself down. She reminded herself that one brief encounter and a night out with eight other people gave her no claim on Blake.

As if he could read her mind, Blake turned away from his conversation and gave her a sexy smile. She was pretty sure she could drown in those dreamy blue eyes of his. Katie suppressed a wistful sigh and tried to think of something to say to him, finding herself speechless once she met his gaze. Blake leaned close enough for Katie to feel the heat coming off of his body and catch a hint of the soap he must have used earlier. She tried to be subtle as she breathed in his intoxicating scent, afraid she might actually swoon.

"You want to dance?" Blake's breath was hot on her ear, and his soft voice sent a delicious shiver down her spine.

"All right," she said, barely able to form the words.

Blake put his glass on the table and pushed his chair back. He cleared his throat. "Excuse us fellas, Miss McCoy and I are going to take a few turns around the dance floor." He winked and took Katie's hand as she rose from her seat.

Katie kept her eyes trained on the concrete floor as she trailed behind Blake, her hand in his. She could practically feel the curious stares on her back as they left, but she didn't trust herself to make eye contact with anyone. The parquet dance floor was crowded with couples, but Blake took Katie's hand and led her into the thick of it. A spirited country song started up, and Blake put one hand on Katie's waist and took her hand with the other. As smoothly as if they had been dancing together for years, he led her around the floor in a two-step with the flow of the crowd. Katie had spent plenty of time on the dance floor, but she had never danced with anyone as charming and confident as Blake.

In his arms, she relaxed and enjoyed the rhythm, the give and take between them, as she looked up into his eyes. His expression was relaxed, like he knew exactly what he was doing. He led her through the dance and never once stepped on her toes or let her bump into another dancer. His hand was warm on her back, strong and masculine. As they twirled around the dance floor, Katie could tell that most of the dancers recognized Blake. He probably didn't get the chance to enjoy himself in public like this very often. Nobody could stop him to ask for an autograph as long as he was moving around the dance floor, though.

The song ended, and a ballad started. Couples left the dance floor and were replaced by others, and before Katie could figure out how to react to the slow song, Blake was pulling her close. Pressed up against his strong, distinctly masculine body, Katie felt light-headed with attraction. Her senses were assaulted and she tightened her grip on him. His spicy, rugged scent surrounded her, his warm body was large and hard against her soft curves, and she could just faintly feel the gentle scratch of his five-o'clock shadow against the top of her head. She was acutely aware of the way his hand felt on her back, the way her breasts were crushed against his chest. Too soon, the song ended, and Blake pulled back.

"You want to get out of here?" People filled the space around them, but Blake made Katie feel like the only person in the world. She didn't know what he had in mind, but when he focused his dark blue eyes on her, she couldn't see or hear anything but him.

"Yes," she managed. She smiled as he took her hand, lacing his fingers through hers.

They walked back to the table where their bands sat and Blake settled the tab for everyone.

"I'm going to walk Miss McCoy back to the hotel. Y'all behave yourselves and don't stay out too late, you hear?" Amusement twinkled in his eyes and he turned back to Katie. "Shall we?" He offered her his arm and she took it.

As they made their way out of the bar, a few fans approached and asked for Blake's autograph or a picture. He obliged them all with a ready smile and an easy nature, but he didn't engage anyone in conversation.

Blake led Katie to the bar's door and out into the hot humid July air, pulling her hand into his. "How far can you walk in those shoes?" Blake asked with a laugh, pointing to Katie's wedge-heeled sandals.

Katie laughed and answered, "They're actually much more comfortable than they look. I'm good for at least a mile or two. The hotel's close, right?"

Blake laughed and nodded. "Yeah, I'll bet you'll be ready to get off your feet once we get inside. I doubt you thought you'd be dancing and then walking home. I guess I could carry you," he teased.

"Don't be silly, Blake. I can make it."

Blake led Katie down the sidewalk past rows of stores, restaurants, and a couple of neighborhood bars. Katie took in the sights and sighed with contentment while she allowed herself to enjoy the delicious way her hand felt in Blake's and the curious stares of the people who realized who he was as they strode past. Blake seemed completely at ease as he led Katie through town, telling her about the guys in his band, asking her what she thought about Sterling's first major show.

In what felt like only a few moments, Katie found herself facing Blake at the door of the hotel where both bands were spending the night. Was this goodnight? Katie wasn't ready for anything serious with Blake, but she didn't want the night to end. Did he think that she was like the groupies that must line up outside his door? Was he expecting her to just drop her panties because he was Blake Jackson, the gorgeous country super star?

He noticed Katie tense up when they reached the hotel and smiled sweetly at her hesitation.

"This is the only private place that we can go right now. My intentions are honorable, and I promise to keep both feet on the floor, Miss McCoy." Blake's gentle teasing and the amusement in his eyes flustered Katie. "We can go our separate ways or maybe see how private the hotel bar is here if you're not comfortable going to my room. It's your choice. No pressure."

"Oh yeah, of course. I didn't think…" Katie stammered. She looked away in embarrassment. Blake laughed softly and opened the heavy glass door of the hotel for her. She stepped inside and said, "I don't mind hanging out in your room for a bit. I'm sure you'll behave yourself."

"Right this way then, darlin'." Blake led Katie to the elevators, his large hand resting on the small of her back.

•••

"Holy cow, *this* is a hotel room! I've never been in one this big." Katie stepped into the cool air-conditioned room and looked around appreciatively.

"Honey, didn't anyone ever tell you that size doesn't matter?" Blake chuckled at his own joke as he closed the door behind him.

Katie giggled and punched him playfully on the shoulder. "Oh you, stop it."

"Darlin', make yourself at home. Grab a drink," Blake gestured to a tub of melting ice and bottled drinks on a marble counter near a giant wicker basket of fruit and wrapped chocolates. Katie couldn't believe the variety. She plucked a fancy-looking bottle of raspberry lemonade out of the slushy ice and wiped it on her jeans. She looked around the luxurious hotel suite, taking in the plush couches positioned close to ornate floor lamps and a tufted leather ottoman in a seating area. Her eyes moved to the bed across the room that sat on a platform, covered in a luxurious looking satin comforter and several fluffy throw pillows. A small crystal chandelier hung over the bed, catching light from the two crystal bedside lamps on the night stands. Katie shook her head a little, forcing herself to take her mind away from Blake's inviting bed.

She perched on Blake's couch and reminded herself to breathe as he crossed the room to join her. He sank down beside her and angled his large frame so that they were facing one another. Blake pushed his boots off his feet and leaned back against the arm of the couch.

"So your show was great. Very impressive," Blake said. "I had only heard one or two of your songs before tonight. I guess it would've been good for me to at least listen to your whole album before y'all joined me, but hearing your stuff for the first time live was a real treat."

"Aw, thanks. Tonight was amazing. I've never experienced anything like it, you know? Our gigs have all been in beer joints or at local fairs. We were so jittery and excited before we went out there tonight. Once we started playing, though, I pretty much forgot to be nervous. It all seemed to just melt into one big ball of energy. Or love. Or something," Katie said with a laugh. "We definitely felt something out there. It was indescribable. Of course you probably know exactly what I'm talking about."

"Sure I do. There's nothing quite like the first time, though," Blake stretched a bit and leaned towards Katie. "Can I have a sip of your drink, sweetheart? I'm too lazy to get up and get my own."

Katie handed over her bottle and looked into Blake's twinkling eyes as he took a big sip. The unexpected intimacy of sharing a drink warmed her. She relaxed and allowed herself to sink back onto the couch. She undid the straps of her sandals and kicked them to the floor, sighing with relief.

Blake chuckled and nodded towards her shoes. "Do you have any shoes that aren't pink?"

"Well, pink is kind of my signature color," Katie replied with a toothy grin.

"I remember those cute pink cowboy boots you were wearing earlier today. I'll bet those are a lot more comfortable."

"They sure are, but sometimes a girl's gotta suffer a bit for the sake of fashion." She winced in pain, and pulled one foot up to massage it.

"Here, allow me," said Blake as he took her foot in his hand and began kneading it for her. Katie sighed with pleasure and allowed herself to lie back on the couch as she watched Blake through lowered lashes.

"This is heaven for me. A girl could get used to this." She reveled in the feel of his warm hands on her tired, achy feet.

"It's my pleasure, darlin'. You have cute little feet." Blake smiled at Katie's obvious enjoyment.

The day's travel, preparation, and show had drained Katie's energy. She was so thankful that they were playing two nights in a row at the same venue. Life on the road might take a bit of getting used to.

Katie felt her eyelids flutter closed as she luxuriated in the soft pressure and steady rhythm of Blake's foot massage. She let herself drift off as she imagined how nice it would feel to sink into a hot bath and then tuck herself between the cool clean sheets of her bed in her hotel room. She hadn't slept on the tour bus yet, but she was pretty sure that it wouldn't be very relaxing. In such tight quarters, each band member would have to be mindful of the others to avoid major tensions on the road.

Sterling had played countless shows, but Orange Blossom, Texas was so close to the Austin clubs where they were usually booked that they had always been able to hit the road in their van. They had played in Louisiana, Oklahoma, and Arkansas as well, but everywhere was within driving distance and they had never been gone long enough to justify the expense of leasing a bus. The bus the label had provided for them for this tour was actually very nice, if a bit crowded, with curtained-off bunks, two lounge areas, and a little kitchen area. The tight quarters and sparse amenities did nothing to dampen Katie's enthusiasm for being on the road, finally touring with a major act.

"...Tuscaloosa?" Blake's voice snapped Katie out of her reverie.

"I'm sorry, what did you say?"

Blake chuckled. "Am I boring you, sweetheart? I just asked if you'd been to Tuscaloosa before. You must be exhausted. I think you would've fallen asleep on this couch if I hadn't woken you. Let me walk you to your room so you can get a little rest. We've got a big day tomorrow." Blake stood up and helped Katie to her feet. His hand lingered at her elbow a bit longer than necessary.

When they reached Katie's room, she fished her room key out of her handbag and looked up into Blake's eyes. "Thank you for tonight, Blake. I had a great time."

"Me, too, Katie; I'd like to do it again soon. You get some sleep tonight, all right? I'll see you tomorrow," he said, his lazy drawl sending a frisson of electricity through Katie. Blake leaned in as if for a kiss but stopped at her forehead where he planted a tender peck before turning and walking back down the hall.

Katie sighed and let herself into the cool sanctuary of her hotel room. With her back against the closed door, she didn't see Blake return, hold up one hand to knock, and pull it back before turning around and heading back to his own room.

Chapter Three

The second day on tour was a blur of activity as the bands were shuffled between interviews and photo sessions. Katie had hoped to spend more time with Blake and maybe build on what they had started the night before, but she barely caught sight of him as the musicians were rushed from one commitment to the next.

Katie attended a band interview for the local paper, smiled and chatted her way through a couple of radio station events, signed autographs, and posed for pictures with fans. She was sure that most of the people crowding around her were more familiar with Blake Jackson, but the publicity was great nonetheless. As the lone female in the band as well as the principal songwriter, Katie generated plenty of interest. Most of the questions Katie answered were about the band, the album, or the tour. Only a handful of people mentioned Blake Jackson, and even fewer actually asked Katie anything about him.

Katie reluctantly headed to her dressing room where the hair and makeup team were waiting. She had hoped to see Blake again and had let thoughts of him distract her all day. Blake had been the first thing she thought of when she woke up and all she had thought of during the day. She had been on edge all day, expecting a phone call or a quick visit with him. That seemed foolish now since he hadn't made any effort to contact her. It was time to get her mind focused on her show, her band, her career.

Tonight's show was important, maybe more important than the last one. Blake had sold out the first night so quickly that they had added a second show to the schedule in Mobile, Alabama.

Katie was certain that fans expected no less than the best and she was determined not to disappoint them. There was no use moping around hoping to catch a glimpse of Blake tonight. It was his tour, and if he wanted to see her, he could have made that happen. She had worked too hard to get to this point in her music career to blow it by losing focus over some guy who apparently hadn't thought of her all day.

She shook her head, blonde locks swishing over her shoulders, and looked herself square in the eyes in the huge dressing room mirror. *Katie McCoy, focus. Tonight you are a star, not a fan of Blake Jackson, not a lovesick teenager. Get it together.*

Katie met her hairstylist's eyes in the mirror and gave her a mischievous smile. "Feel free to go crazy and try something sexy. I wouldn't mind looking amazing tonight," Katie laughed. She looked to her makeup artist and quipped, "That goes double for you." The stylists laughed and voiced their approval. With one show down and only eleven to go before Sterling left Blake Jackson's tour, Katie had to make every night count. This tour could be very important for her music career, and lord knows she needed everything to go well. Katie had finished high school, but she never went to college and so far had never done anything else well besides write and play music.

If things didn't work out with Sterling, maybe she could join another band. If worse came to worst, Katie could move back in with her parents and teach private music lessons. After getting a little taste of life as a successful musician, though, Katie wouldn't give it up without a fight. Every show on this tour was a chance to promote the album, gain new fans, live her dream, and maybe catch Blake's eye while she was at it. She might be reading too much into her brief encounters with Blake, but there was a chance that he felt the same sparks flying that she did.

When her hair and makeup team stepped back to admire their work, Katie took a long, appreciative look at her reflection. She had been surprised by the transformation last night, but that was nothing compared to the beautiful creature staring back at her in the mirror.

"You two are amazing! You might as well be magicians, ladies. I don't think that I've ever looked this good," Katie gushed to the hairstylist and makeup artist. "Thank you so much." Katie hugged the two women and headed out to meet the band. *It's show time,* she thought to herself.

• • •

While Katie was busy trying to get her mind off of Blake, Blake was thinking of nothing but Katie. He closed his eyes and let the hot water of his shower run down his back as he breathed in the steam and tried to wash away the day's work and ready himself for that night's show. His day had been filled with press commitments and fan events, and neither had been easy to focus on when all he wanted to do was whisk little Miss Katie McCoy into a quiet room and spend a little time getting to know her. He regretted not kissing her outside her hotel room the night before and hoped to get another chance soon.

Blake couldn't think of anything but her beautiful face, that silky blonde hair, those glittering green eyes, those rosebud lips. Why hadn't he kissed her last night? He had certainly wanted to, and it seemed like she would have been receptive. Blake tried to think of one other time when a woman had distracted him so much and came up short. He felt like a teenager when it came to Katie, a feeling he wasn't entirely comfortable with. Blake was used to a lot of female attention from fans, and he was usually at ease, practically in his element when he met a new woman. He never saw any of them as a potential girlfriend, though. It was too hard to maintain a relationship when he toured most of the year, and when he was home, no woman was willing to sit on the sidelines while he spent his days and nights writing and recording albums.

Maybe Katie could fit into his life, since she would certainly understand the stresses and demands of an active music career. Katie could be someone special, and that was scary. Scary, but enticing. This might require more than just the patented Blake Jackson charm, the lazy smile, the little jokes he generally relied on. The regular playbook might not be enough when it came to someone like Katie.

•••

Another amazing performance left Katie in high spirits, and she practically floated back to her dressing room. She thought that the band was tight before they joined the tour. The shows they played in the clubs and bars around Texas were nothing compared to the size and production involved on this tour. She couldn't wait to see what the rest of the tour held, and was so glad that the band had managed to get these dates. Opening for Blake Jackson was going to put Sterling in front of thousands of fans, many of which had likely never heard of them. It was the chance of a lifetime, and she had to admit that she was more than a little relieved to find that they were holding up under the pressure of performing for bigger audiences than ever before.

She let herself into her dressing room and relished the whoosh of cool air that greeted her. Her jaw dropped when she stepped inside and saw a huge arrangement of pink roses sitting in a vase on her vanity. Were these from Blake? Her heartbeat quickened but she reminded herself that her sweet parents also knew exactly where she was and might just be sending their love. She plucked the card from amongst the leaves and sucked in her breath as she read the words.

Katie, You looked and sounded incredible tonight. I hope you'll come to my show. There's a seat backstage saved just for you. Yours, Blake.

She turned the card over in her fingers a couple of times and pressed it to her lips. She allowed herself a moment to close her eyes and imagine what it would feel like to kiss Blake, his lips warm and soft on hers, before she snapped to attention and got herself ready for his show. With her heart racing, Katie rushed through a shower and changed into clean clothes so she could make it on time to see Blake's set.

• • •

Katie made her way to the backstage audience area, which was nothing more than a couple of rows of metal folding chairs and was actually more off to the side than the back of the stage. She had often wondered why people were so keen on getting to sit backstage, since the view was so limited and the sound was off. She guessed it was the allure of being granted special status, since it certainly wasn't for the ambience or the view of the show. She found the seating area and saw that one of the chairs had a card with her name printed on it in bold letters and a single yellow rose waiting for her on the seat. She hurried to her seat as the house lights dimmed and the stage lights began to blaze. She brought the flower to her nose and inhaled deeply.

Blake paused by her chair when the band walked in and gently pulled her up from her chair. He drew her hand to his lips and kissed her knuckles, his eyes never leaving hers. "I'm glad you made it." His breath on her hand gave her a delicious thrill. Blake released her hand and ran up the steps and onto the stage.

Katie's legs wobbled under her as she stood rooted in place, staring dreamily after Blake. The music started, the crowd went wild, and she became peripherally aware that everyone around her was staring. She sat down in her chair in a daze, intoxicated by her brief moment with Blake. Her face reddened as she slowly looked at the curious faces surrounding her. The small seating area was full of friends and family of the band members, contest winners, and staff members. Everyone had witnessed their exchange, noticed the special treatment, and looked like they wondered what was going on between Blake and the young fiddler.

She soon forgot to be self-conscious as the band played on and Blake's dreamy voice filled the auditorium. Katie sat, mesmerized, as Blake sang the songs she had heard a hundred times before. She knew all of his songs by heart, could play most of them herself, in fact; but tonight they sounded new to her; it was as if she were under his spell. His warm voice made everything around her fade away as he sang; she couldn't think of anything else but him.

She was momentarily jolted from her daze when Blake introduced his popular song 'Someone Like You', looked over at her, made purposeful eye contact, and told the crowd that the song suddenly had new meaning for him. Katie had to employ every last ounce of her self-control to remain upright in her chair after that. Was he playing with her? Was he flirting, trying to send a real message, or just working the crowd? If only she could get a few moments alone with him after the show, maybe he would give her a better idea.

Both Sterling and Blake had fan meet and greet events after the show, and Katie had to be satisfied with no more than occasional glimpses of Blake. There was no way they would have any conversation that night, private or otherwise. Knowing that he was in charge and could delay the fan events to see her, but chose not to, was tough to take. Katie knew that she shouldn't be upset. He wasn't avoiding her; this was work, and he was a professional. Blake didn't get to where he was by upsetting fans and skipping commitments. He had caught her eye a couple of times, but she could never tell if it was coincidence or if he was thinking of her, trying to send a message.

Chapter Four

Katie looked out the window of Sterling's tour bus as they left Mobile behind. In a little over three hours, they would arrive in Tuscaloosa, Alabama, where they would actually have a full day off before taking the stage the next evening. After the Tuscaloosa show, the tour schedule would pick up and there would be much less downtime between stops. Sterling had joined Blake's tour during a slow period, and Katie couldn't let herself get used to the leisurely pace.

Her band had spent several months in the past playing night after night with little time off between gigs, but they had always gone home or to a hotel afterwards. Sleeping on a tour bus was going to be much different. Each band member had their own private bunk, but only a curtain separated the beds from the open area of the bus. Everything was designed to make the most of the limited space, so there was no bathtub, only a shower; no full size refrigerator, only one that would be at home in a dorm room; nothing like the comforts of home. Sterling's recent success had been such a whirlwind ride, such an exhilarating experience that none of it mattered. Getting their own tour bus was a huge step, such a sign of their success that they were too excited to grouse about the cramped quarters. Besides, the shows and fan events were so exhausting that the little bunks felt like heaven when the musicians fell into bed at night.

Katie sat back on a small black leather sofa in the front lounge area of the bus and admired her flowers. She wouldn't be able to keep them for long; she had propped them up in the tiny kitchen sink for the ride to Tuscaloosa and it was only a matter of time before they'd have to be moved. Just seeing them made her smile as she let her thoughts run free, remembering the feel of Blake's warm lips on her hand the night before, wondering what those lips would feel like pressed against her own.

As soon as the bus left the parking lot that morning, her band mates had descended upon her in the bus's lounge area and subjected Katie to intense questioning about Blake, what was going on, and why she was getting such special treatment from the star. She had seen genuine concern in their eyes amidst their good-natured promises to put him in his place if he hurt her. The band was used to guarding her, always on alert for signs of trouble, as though she were their personal responsibility. They worried for her and didn't relax until they knew that she was safe. She assured the men that she had only had a few casual encounters with Blake and that nothing had really happened.

Katie didn't mention how much she wanted something to happen, though. She didn't tell the guys that her world stopped whenever Blake was around, that the sound of his voice promised a beautiful forever, or that when he touched her hand she wasn't entirely sure that her feet were on the ground. For the first time since she had joined Sterling, Katie began to wish that there was another female member. The guys were great but it would be nice to have someone to talk with about Blake.

Katie's cell phone rang and she snapped to attention. She didn't recognize the number but answered.

"Katie?" Blake's deep voice was unmistakable.

"How did you get my number?" Katie teased. Her tension melted away as she sank back down into her seat when she realized that it was Blake on the line.

"Honey, I had my people ask your people. You might want to consider a change in personnel. It was pretty easy to get your information," Blake replied with a laugh. "You guys on your way to Tuscaloosa yet?"

"We've been on the road about thirty minutes."

"We're just a little bit ahead of you, then. I'm calling to see if you'd like to have dinner with me tonight."

"You mean like a date?" Katie asked. The conversations around her seemed to stop and everyone on the bus listened while they pretended not to listen.

"That's exactly what I mean, darlin'. I know a great place in Tuscaloosa and I'd love to take you out tonight," Blake said. Katie could hear the smile in his voice and closed her eyes as she imagined how sexy he must look. She pictured him relaxing on his own bus, maybe a little stubble covering his cheeks.

"I'd love to," she said. Katie thought she should try to play it cool but found that she just couldn't hide her feelings from Blake, nor did she want to. She wasn't going to move too fast with him, but with a little less than three weeks together there was no time for games.

"Well, all right. I imagine we'll roll into town around three this afternoon. I'll give you some time to do whatever you need to do and I'll come by and grab you at six. Does that sound okay?"

"Sounds perfect," Katie answered.

"Great, see you then. Enjoy the ride," Blake said and then hung up.

Katie was dazed as she put her phone down and looked around the bus. Had Blake Jackson—THE Blake Jackson—really just officially asked her out? On a real live date? She squealed and did a little happy dance as she stood up and made her way to the little refrigerator across from the couch. She grabbed a cold bottle of water and pressed it to her forehead, took a deep breath, and centered herself. *So Blake Jackson asked me out. He's sweet and we get along great. This should be fun. No big deal. It's just a date.*

Katie sat back down on the little sofa by the window and stared at the blank screen on the bus's plasma TV. Now what? Before the phone call, Katie had worked so hard at convincing herself not to let her imagination run wild. A few sweet encounters did not mean that she and Blake had some romantic future ahead of them. Letting herself get excited over a couple of conversations and one gorgeous flower arrangement could set her up for major disappointment if she fell for Blake and he had simply been passing time being friendly to the lone girl in the opening band. His phone call asking her for a date changed everything, didn't it? He wouldn't ask her out if he didn't like her too, right? Now if only she could manage to make it through a dinner without acting like a crazed fan or blurting out something stupid. She needed a distraction. Three hours on the road was long enough to work herself into quite a lather over her upcoming date.

Katie was thinking of popping in a DVD, kicking back, and shutting off her mind for an hour or so when Charles Cranston, Sterling's singer, ambled through the bus's short hallway and into the front lounge area. Charles dropped down onto the sofa opposite Katie and opened a bottle of water.

"So. You and Blake Jackson, huh?" Charles sipped his drink and eyed Katie with amusement.

Katie laughed. "It's just dinner, Charles. He's probably just being nice. I'm sure it doesn't mean anything."

"Well, honey, I notice that he didn't invite the whole band, just you. If I didn't know better, I'd say that you are going on an actual, real-life date tonight. Just try not to forget about me when you two fall in love and run away together."

"Ha! I don't think you need to worry about that. I doubt we'll even see each other once we go back home. I don't think much can happen in a couple of weeks, especially a couple of weeks on a major tour. We'll both be too busy with the tour to fall in love, much less run away together. I mean, when would we have the time?" Katie giggled.

"You'd be surprised at how much can happen in a couple of weeks, sweetheart. Being on tour is a bit like being in a pressure cooker. The conditions are perfect, and relationships can develop a lot faster than normal. I've been in this business a long time, and I've seen crazier things happen. Just be careful, you know, remember who you are, and you can have fun without getting hurt. Blake seems like a good guy, but you should still take care of yourself. Being on the road can make people do crazy things." Charles stood up and stretched. "I think I'm going to grab a little shuteye before we roll into Tuscaloosa. Wake me when we get there, OK?"

"All right. You could use the beauty sleep anyway," Katie said with a wink. She watched Charles climb into his bunk and pull the curtain closed. She smiled and shook her head. A relationship pressure cooker, huh? Charles was always dispensing wisdom about love, life, and music.

Without a distraction, Katie would drive herself crazy with anxiety over her upcoming date. It was too early to start getting ready, she was too fidgety to write a song or take a nap, so she decided to watch a movie. She fished her copy of *Miss Congeniality* out of the bin of DVDs and headed for her own bunk. A couple of hours propped up in her bed with her favorite movie would help her relax and forget about Blake, at least for a while.

Katie climbed into her bunk and closed the curtain, relishing the privacy, or at least the semblance of privacy, of the small space. She pulled her personal DVD player screen down from the roof of her compartment and started the movie. She breathed a contented sigh as she leaned back and tried to let Sandra Bullock take her mind off of Blake for a couple of hours. She'd be in Tuscaloosa soon enough and would have plenty of time to stress out before her date with Blake tonight.

Her date! What would she wear? Who would do her hair and makeup? She would be on her own this time. What would Blake think of everyday Katie, without professionally styled hair and expertly applied makeup? Oh God, he was going to realize what a nobody she really was, wasn't he?

• • •

Katie perched nervously on the edge of the tour bus's small leather sofa, checked her watch, and willed her leg to stop bouncing. The bus had arrived in Tuscaloosa and Katie had managed to get herself ready for the date on the bus, no easy feat. Normally, when a band arrived in town they secured a hotel room for the driver. He would sleep during the day and be ready to drive at night, and the band members could use the shower in that room in the meantime. There hadn't been enough time to get the room secured, so Katie had to get ready on board the bus.

Her band mates had given her plenty of grief over the way the steam from her shower had perfumed the bus, how the outfits she rejected for the date were strewn over her bunk, and how her makeup was all over the table in the front lounge. Their teasing had embarrassed her, but now that she was alone in the bus, everyone else having gone off to find entertainment, she wished that the guys were still with her. At least their good-natured ribbing had distracted her enough to forget how nervous she was for a little while. Blake was due to collect her soon, but now the minutes were dragging by and her nerves were keeping her on edge.

Katie's heart jumped into her throat at the sound of Blake's soft knock on the bus's door. She got to her feet, not completely sure that her legs would carry her in her frazzled state, and made her way to the door to greet him. She took the hand that he offered to help her walk down the steps and wondered if he felt the same jolt of electric attraction that she felt when their skin touched.

Blake looked down at Katie and kissed her forehead softly. He breathed in the scent of her hair and said, "Hey beautiful. It's good to see you again." His voice was husky and his dark blue eyes were intense.

"Hey yourself," said Katie. "It's good to see you too." She felt a lump form in her throat as she met his gaze then looked away, scanning the parking lot. "Did you drive?"

"That's me over there," he said, pointing to a black Mercedes Benz S Class. "My assistant arranged a rental for me while we're in town. Shall we?" Blake offered his hand and Katie took it. She grinned up at him when he gave her hand a little squeeze. He opened her car door for her and waited while she slid into the luxurious leather seat before closing it for her.

"I've never been in a car this nice before," Katie said as she looked around the vehicle's interior. The car's air conditioner blew deliciously cool air on her face, and Katie's heart squeezed a little when she realized that her band's CD was playing. Blake Jackson had a copy of her band's album! And he was listening to it!

"Yeah, it's a pretty sweet ride, I guess. I prefer something a little more practical myself. I drive a pickup at home."

"Where's home?" Katie angled herself so that she could face him a little better as Blake pulled out of the parking lot and into traffic. She enjoyed the opportunity to indulge herself and stare at him without interruption. His face looked freshly shaven, and the hair behind his ears was still a little damp. He might be as excited about their date as she was.

"Nashville. My parents and older brother still live in Knoxville, where I grew up, but I moved out to Nashville as soon as I got serious about music. I love Knoxville, but at the time, I couldn't see a way to really make it in country music without hitting Nashville. That's where all the talent seems to get discovered. It paid off, I guess. Maybe I can take you to my place when we get to town. I haven't been home in a couple of months but I have a guy who helps keep everything at the house running smoothly."

"I'd love to see your house, Blake. That would be really nice," said Katie as she lowered her eyes shyly. It was hard not to get ahead of herself when everything he said sounded so cozy and romantic to her.

"So you guys are from Orange Blossom, huh? I've actually got a little place out in Austin. I don't get down there as much as I'd like, but I love it when I'm there, unless it's summer, of course. I don't know how you Texans stand that heat, it's so brutal," he said. "I'm surprised that I never caught one of your shows. I love the music scene in Austin, and I'm sure y'all played all over that town." Blake glanced over at Katie and grinned before training his eyes back on the road. She loved watching the muscles ripple in his tan forearms as he drove.

"Yeah, we pretty much play anywhere that will have us. There are quite a few bars and clubs in the smaller towns around Austin that are always glad to have cheap live music, but it's a little tougher to make it in Austin. Short of moving to Nashville, Austin's our best bet for exposure. It was worth the trouble, though, you know? Look at us now, opening on a big time tour." Katie giggled.

"Yep, look at you now." Blake smiled at Katie indulgently, fond amusement dancing in his eyes. "Does your family live in Orange Blossom?"

"Yes, well, my parents do. I'm an only child. My folks have been there forever; I don't think they'll ever leave. My dad has the only optometry practice in town, and my mother is practically an institution. I don't think there's a person in town who doesn't know her."

"Sounds like my folks. They've been in Knoxville forever. So you're an only child, huh? I can't imagine what that's like. I have an older brother, so I've never been the only one."

"Well, I think that they would've liked to have had another child, but it just never happened."

• • •

Blake pulled the Mercedes into the parking lot of a small, unassuming restaurant, Evangeline's. "We're here, darlin'. Hope you're hungry." Blake hopped out and rushed to open Katie's door for her. She giggled at his exaggerated strides as he made his way around the car. He offered his hand as she pulled herself out of the car, knowing that she didn't need help maneuvering herself but unwilling to pass up the chance to hold her hand.

Blake opened the restaurant door, and Katie stepped inside. The couple was greeted immediately by a hostess who was obviously flustered and star struck, but trying to act natural. "Welcome to Evangeline's. Table for two?" She said.

"Yes, ma'am," Blake looked at the hostess's nametag, "Elizabeth. We should have a reservation for six-thirty. Bl-"

"Blake Jackson. I know who you are, sir." Elizabeth flushed bright red. "Sorry for interrupting." She lowered her voice to a stage whisper and said, "I mean I know who you are. We have a private table for you and your date. Right this way." Elizabeth led Blake and Katie through the restaurant to a dim corner table partially shielded from the dining room by a decorative column. "Meredith will be your server this evening. Enjoy your meal."

"Thank you, Elizabeth," said Blake as he pressed a folded twenty-dollar bill into the surprised hostess's palm. With a grateful smile, Elizabeth left and Blake and Katie were alone again.

"I come here every time I make it to Tuscaloosa. They know me here," Blake said.

"I'll admit, I am kind of surprised that we were able to walk all the way to the table without anyone stopping you," Katie answered.

"I usually make it through my meals here without any attention. Seems like half the time if I just leave my boots and cowboy hat at home nobody knows who I am, or at least if they do they realize that I'm here for dinner and they leave me be. Could just be that it's not really a country music crowd or something," Blake replied. "So, what are you in the mood for, sweetheart? Pretty much everything is good here."

"Hmm, let's see. I think I'll have anything but another sandwich. Since joining this tour I've eaten more sandwiches than ever before in my life!"

"Yeah, that's the truth. Seems like every venue catering menu is the same, sandwiches, cold cuts, cheese cubes. Enough with the cheese cubes already," Blake said with a smile.

They ordered their meals and a bottle of red wine to share, and Blake watched Katie as much as he could without staring. He wondered if her hair felt as soft as it looked, what her slender arms would feel like wrapped around his shoulders, and what her full lips would feel like on his. Her eyes danced as she shared stories of her band's earliest gigs, and Blake found himself riveted. He had been in the music business a long time and had pretty much heard and seen it all. Somehow her stories sounded fresh to him, though. Everything about her was a breath of fresh air. Her hearty laugh surprised him when he was lucky enough to amuse her. It was surprising that something so robust could come from such a petite girl.

Plenty about Katie McCoy surprised Blake. He knew that she was a beautiful and talented musician, and that was enough, but when she mentioned that she wrote most of Sterling's lyrics and collaborated on most of the band's music, Blake nearly choked on his food.

"You're the songwriter?" Blake was impressed.

"Well yeah, mostly. Charles, our singer, and I collaborate on a bunch of them, but I usually come up with the bulk of the lyrics.

I pretty much imagine what I would want to hear from a guy and go from there. The guys really like having the female perspective. If it were left up to them, all our songs would be about drinking beer, driving trucks, and hanging out."

"Hey you know, I think a lot of country music is like that. Honey, I'm impressed. I'll be listening to your songs with a new appreciation now." Blake looked at Katie with new respect and admiration. "So you're gorgeous, talented, and sweet. What's wrong with you? What are you hiding?" Blake asked in a kidding tone.

A startled look flew across her lovely features, and before Blake could be sure of what he had seen, she rearranged her face into a coy conspiratorial smile. "Well…I'm a horrible cook, I'm kind of a slob, and I'm a bad kisser," Katie said. She leaned forward on her elbows and gave Blake a meaningful look.

"I don't believe a word you say," whispered Blake as he leaned in and brushed his lips against hers. He felt her shudder as he took her face in his hands and pressed his lips to hers. The world around him faded away as he coaxed her lips open with his tongue and gently deepened the kiss, exploring her mouth, moving his hands to cradle her head and hold her closer. He breathed in the sweet scent of her hair mingled with her fresh perfume, feeling intoxicated by her scent, her soft hair in his hands, her kiss.

He pulled his head back and looked into her eyes, noticing that she looked as dazed as he felt. "You lied," Blake said, as he tried to regain his composure, hoping that their kiss had gone unnoticed by their fellow diners.

"What?" Katie looked so bewildered that Blake almost regretted his joke.

"You lied about being a bad kisser, honey. That was one of the best kisses of my life," Blake explained.

"Oh, me too, Blake. That was amazing." Blake thought she looked relieved.

"Is everything okay, darlin'?" Blake's eyes searched Katie's face.

"Of—of course Blake. What do you mean?"

"Well, for starters, we just shared an amazing kiss and while I feel like I found my bliss, you look like you're about to jump out of your skin. What gives?" Blake teased gently, real concern in his eyes.

"It's nothing. I'm fine. Really."

Blake took Katie's hand and focused his eyes on hers. "Katie McCoy. If you say it's nothing then I will believe you, but if it's something, I hope you know that you can tell me anything."

Katie took a deep breath, and admitted, "I guess it's not exactly nothing."

"I know that we just met, but I want you to feel like you can talk to me. If you have a problem, I would like to help you. I think you can trust me."

Katie took a deep breath and stared at her hands, clenched into fists in her lap. She let the breath out and began, "I just can't help but to think about what's going to happen when we're done with your tour. On one hand, I really like you and I don't want to miss a single moment. On the other hand, I feel like I should be careful so I don't have my heart broken when I have to go home."

Blake gave her a gentle smile. "I know, darlin'. Relationships have never been my strong point. I don't know what will happen between us, what *can* happen, in three weeks, but I just figured we'd ride it out and see. We don't have to decide now, and we definitely don't need to worry about anything just yet. Let's just have some fun together and see what happens."

• • •

Katie felt foolish for admitting her fears, for opening up so soon, for assuming so much. She had such a poor track record when it came to relationships. No boyfriend had made it past a month or two with her, so she was beginning to wonder if she was the problem. She'd find a nice guy, get to know him, and then before she knew it they were breaking up. The common denominator in these discussions was the band, how much time it took, how often she went away for gigs, what she was doing when she was on the road. Guys couldn't manage to be supportive without being jealous and she always had to cut them loose.

Now here she was sitting across from a gorgeous man, having just shared an amazing kiss, and she's already worried about how they're going to end things? What was she doing? Blake Jackson was the country's biggest star. She should consider herself lucky to be on this date, should just enjoy it while she could. He probably thought she was a basket case.

Chapter Five

Katie woke up the next morning feeling more tired than when she had fallen into bed the night before. Replaying her date with Blake in her mind over and over again as she lie in bed kept her up, unable to fall asleep. The kiss had been magic, pure magic. She couldn't remember ever having felt so close to someone that she had just met, and not knowing if Blake felt the same was killing her. Was she a distraction for him? A fling to keep his mind (and lips) occupied while he was on the road? Or did he feel the pull, the draw, towards her like she did to him? Would he take the time to get to know her or be like every other guy she met and want to take things straight to the bedroom?

Katie had met her share of guys interested in only one thing, and it wasn't her budding music career. Why couldn't she find someone who supported her dreams and didn't make her feel guilty for pursuing her goals? She had never wanted anything more than to make a career with her music, and this tour was the best way to move that forward. Distracting herself with Blake wasn't going to get her anywhere. The guys on the bus were beginning to stir, so she pulled herself together and pasted a smile on her face. It was time to focus on the men in her life who wanted the same things she did.

• • •

Katie jumped at the knock on her dressing room door. "Yes?" Her sleepless night had caught up with her and she was dozing on her little couch, trying to rest up for that night's show.

"It's me, Katie." Blake's muffled voice answered.

"Come on in." She sat up on the couch and ran her fingers through her hair.

Blake closed the door quietly behind him and crossed the room to join Katie on her couch, his eyes dancing and his expression warm. He sat next to her and chuckled. "Looks like I woke somebody up."

She yawned and stretched. "I must have drifted off. I was just resting up a little before it was time to get ready for tonight."

"Sweetheart, I didn't think it was possible, but you look even cuter when you're sleepy." Blake held a strand of Katie's hair between his fingers before tucking it behind her ear.

"You are too sweet, Mr. Jackson." Katie cast her eyes down demurely at the compliment. Already, being on tour with Blake had pushed them into situations where they normally wouldn't have seen each other for weeks or months into the relationship. Charles was right, being tour was like being in a pressure cooker. Everything was moving faster than in what Katie considered the real world. Her worries last night of what he would think of her without professional hair and makeup seemed silly now that he was seeing her just moments after waking up. Her sleep-mussed hair and bare face must present quite the picture.

"So, I keep thinking about you, about our kiss last night. I have a couple of interviews and a meet and greet thing with some radio station contest winners, but I couldn't resist stopping in to see you first. I was hoping that we could take a few minutes to hang out, but I gotta tell you, I don't think I can keep my hands off of you." Blake pulled Katie into his arms and ran his fingers through her hair. He inhaled deeply, his nose at the top of her head, and she could feel the warmth coming off his skin as her lips grazed his neck. Katie allowed herself to relax in the warmth of Blake's comforting embrace. If only she could stay here in his arms forever and just forget about everything else. It would be so easy to ignore the deadline looming ahead, to pretend that they had all the time in the world to be together.

She wished she could take her time with Blake, to get to know him and let him discover her secrets, before they had to decide whether to go their separate ways or find a way to be together. The problem was that he already felt so much like he could belong to her. Being in his arms was exciting, thrilling, but it also felt like it was where she had always belonged. It was like coming home, and the thought of leaving him at the end of the tour terrified her.

He held her close in his strong, solid embrace and she breathed in his clean, masculine scent. She looked up into his face and saw tenderness mingled with desire in his eyes. He leaned down and pressed his lips to hers, cupped her face in his hands, and kissed her again. Blake drew back and Katie saw a fiery passion that matched her own burning in his eyes. He kissed her forehead, each cheek in turn, and returned to her mouth to plant a firm, insistent kiss on her lips. He deepened the kiss as she arched her body to meet his. Katie's senses were reeling. Her body was tingling, her blood zinging with electricity as Blake's kiss worked its magic. She was hypnotized, intoxicated by his passion, and the world fell away around her as her body responded to his.

Blake drew back, his hands still cupping her face, and searched her eyes. "Katie," he breathed.

Katie felt drugged from the kiss, as if she were floating. "Blake," she responded.

"You don't know what you do to me." He looked as affected by the kiss as she was. When their eyes met, understanding flowed between them, and she knew she could never let him go.

• • •

The hair and makeup team arrived, ready to transform Katie for the show. She tried to focus on getting ready and let them do their jobs while they shared gossip and swooned over a cute new security team member they had passed on their way through the venue to Katie's dressing room. Their girlish giggles brought a reluctant smile to Katie's face as they rhapsodized over his gorgeous muscular body, his sexy deep voice, and his beautiful blue eyes.

She was clearly being too serious about Blake and their imminent separation. It had been too long since she had been excited by a new guy, and her fretting was threatening to ruin the whole thing. Here she was, actually living her dream of being on a major country artist's tour, and she was spending all her time worrying about how she was going to feel in a few weeks when she had to go home. She should try to relax a little, might as well enjoy the tour while it lasted.

Chapter Six

The tour schedule heated up as the buses rolled through the Alabama tour stops and into Tennessee. Sterling had been together for six years, since Katie was a newly-minted eighteen year-old high school graduate, but they had never before spent so much time together without a break from one another.

The guys in the band had noticed how much attention Katie was getting from Blake Jackson, but if it bothered them, nobody said anything. She wasn't sure if she was just being touchy, but it seemed like they might come to resent her for the special treatment. As it was, everybody on board their bus was snappish with each other, and nobody was getting along. It was disappointing, really, to not be able to enjoy the tour when it would be over so soon.

The tension on the Sterling tour bus was thick when Blake called. Katie accepted his invitation for dinner in Knoxville as soon as the question left his lips.

"Yes, I'd love to. I gotta get out of here!" she said breathlessly.

"Well, darlin', I think I'm just going to let myself believe that you're excited to see me. I'd hate to think that I'm just an easy means of escape," Blake laughed good-naturedly.

"Of course I'm looking forward to seeing you. I'm just also looking forward to getting a break from the guys. They're not exactly my biggest fans these days. I think we'll all benefit from a little break from one another. Where are we going?"

"That, my dear, is a surprise. Just relax and don't worry your pretty little head about it, sweetheart. You'll find out when I pick you up at six." With that, Blake ended the call, leaving Katie smiling and giddy with anticipation. She and Blake hadn't been on a proper date since the dinner in Tuscaloosa. They had been forced to settle for stolen moments in dressing rooms, nights out with the bands, and phone calls. She couldn't complain, though; it was an unconventional courtship, but every moment with Blake had been a dream come true.

During those stolen encounters, Katie had pieced together an understanding of Blake. It wasn't the ideal way to get to know someone, but it worked. She found that she had to force herself to focus on the tour, to be present when she was with her band. Every moment they were apart, Katie felt the pull towards Blake, found her mind wandering, wondering what he was doing and reliving a kiss or an embrace. They had certainly made the most of their moments together, sharing kisses and secrets, getting to know one another. Going out on a real date would be a special treat tonight, and six o'clock couldn't come soon enough.

Katie rifled through her luggage to find something to wear on her mystery date, hoping that if she needed to dress a certain way that Blake would have told her. She settled on a cute casual outfit and concentrated her efforts on her hair and makeup.

•••

Katie forgot her worries of being underdressed in her skirt and simple top when they pulled into the parking lot of Betty's, a rustic-looking restaurant advertising Knoxville's best home cooking. A wraparound porch housed large rocking chairs and whiskey barrel flower planters. An elderly man wearing denim overalls and a red baseball cap rocked slowly back and forth in one of the chairs and offered a friendly wave and toothy grin to Blake and Katie as they climbed the steps toward the door.

The pair entered the bustling restaurant and Blake received shouted greetings, hearty handshakes, and playful pats on the back. As Katie's eyes adjusted to the restaurant's dim interior, she noticed peanut shells covering the smooth cement floor, a knotty pine bar lined with rugged-looking men in work shirts and trucker hats, neon beer signs, and a large table in the corner where a family sat, looking at them excitedly. Katie hid her bewilderment behind a smile as Blake took her hand and led her purposefully towards the smiling family.

Her confusion grew as a woman and two men who looked somehow familiar stood and hurried towards Blake, where they wrapped him in a fierce group hug. The woman was kissing Blake's cheek while the older man held onto Blake's hand, the younger man having stepped back. Blake moved back towards Katie and put an arm around her waist. "Mom, Dad, this is Katie McCoy. Katie, meet Betty and Roy Jackson."

"Wow, hi, what a surprise! It's so nice to meet you," said Katie as she moved forward to shake hands with Betty Jackson and was enveloped in a soft, cinnamon-scented hug instead.

The younger man stepped forward and put his hand out to Katie. "I'm Luke, Blake's older and much wiser brother. He must have forgotten his manners." Luke smiled at Katie with a twinkle in his blue eyes as his warm hand held hers.

"It's so nice to meet you," said Katie, trying to recover from her shock.

"Honey, Blake told us you were pretty. He didn't tell us you were gorgeous! Y'all sit down and we'll get some supper," insisted Betty as she led the group back to the family's table.

Katie struggled to regain her composure as she sat at the table with Blake's family. Meeting the parents was such a big step, something she didn't realize that they were ready for. Now that it was happening, it felt right. Katie and Blake had known each other such a short time, but they didn't have a lot of time to waste when it came down to it. In a couple of weeks they would go their separate ways, Katie back home to Orange Blossom, Blake on to the rest of the tour. It seemed a little soon to meet the family, but why not? With such a short time left together, why not indulge the fantasy? Why not suspend reality a bit and forget about the deadline looming ahead?

Blake rubbed Katie's thigh under the table and leaned close to whisper to her, "Sorry about the ambush, sweetheart. I think they really like you though." Any irritation she might have felt about the surprise melted away at his touch.

Katie gazed into Blake's eyes. "This is quite a surprise, but it's nice."

"You two must be starving. What do they feed you on this tour? Let's get some supper." Betty motioned for a waitress. Katie was charmed by Betty's motherly concern with the care and feeding of one of the country's biggest stars.

"Katie, you gotta try the pot roast. They use Betty's mama's recipe, and it is delicious. You're not a vegetarian or anything, are you? Blake told me you were from Texas." Roy leaned over and smiled at Katie as he spoke, blue eyes dancing. *Those Jackson boys and their blue eyes,* thought Katie.

"No, sir, I'm not a vegetarian. I'd love to try the pot roast, but how do they have Betty's mom's recipe?" Katie asked.

Luke laughed. "They've got all of her best recipes, and most of Mom's, too. This is my parents' restaurant," he explained as he gestured to Betty and Roy. "Yes, it's sad but true. Blake Jackson's parents still have to work." A joking smile played on his lips.

"Katie, don't listen to him. I always wanted to run a restaurant, but of course in the early days we could never afford to open our own place. Blake was kind enough to put up the money for this joint a couple of years ago and we've been happily running it ever since." Betty gave Blake a fond look.

"Oh, you own this place? How cool is that?" Katie loved that Blake had bought his parents a restaurant. They didn't seem old enough to retire, didn't really seem the type to want to live off of their famous son, and they were certainly at home in this restaurant of their own.

"It's pretty cool, Katie. Any time I can get away for lunch, I can come in and get a free meal," Luke chimed in.

Blake took Katie's hand and explained, "My folks wanted Luke to wait tables or tend bar here, but he was too busy going to medical school. Now he's a big-time doctor here in town, and too busy running a charitable foundation and his own practice. They make sure kids in the more rural areas of Tennessee have access to vaccinations and routine health screenings. They go out, set up clinics, and make sure parents know what's available. Sometimes he gets so busy that he forgets to eat lunch. Mom only feeds him here so he won't waste away."

Luke laughed and turned to Katie, "It's true, I'm a big-time doctor. I'm also very single, in case you have any pretty friends." He waggled his eyebrows as Katie giggled. *Single and handsome,* she thought, *almost as good-looking as Blake.*

"I'll keep that in mind Luke," Katie responded with an indulgent smile. "You know, my dad is an optometrist. He's the only one in Orange Blossom. What kind of medicine do you practice?"

"I'm a general practitioner. I have a family practice in Knoxville with a partner. He runs the foundation with me as well."

"That's very cool. Now I know who to call if I get sick in Tennessee." Katie gave Luke a warm smile and thought how proud Roy and Betty must be of their boys. She wondered if her parents wished she had gone to medical school or something more prestigious than joining a band right out of high school. They had never said anything about her skipping college, working at bars to pay her bills, or even having to pick up shifts at her father's practice when money was tight. They had been so supportive of her efforts with Sterling that without their help, she would've had to drop out of the band long before the six years it had taken them to get their big break.

The food arrived and everyone tucked in to the steaming plates of meatloaf, pot roast, chicken fried steak, and pork chops. Katie took a bite of the pot roast Roy had recommended and closed her eyes, savoring the flavor. She couldn't eat like this every day and still hope to fit into her tour wardrobe, but for tonight it was perfect, each bite a piece of heaven. If it weren't for the myriad conversations around them, it would be easy to imagine sitting around the dining room table at home, enjoying home cooking with Blake's family.

Luke wiped his mouth with a napkin and faced Katie. "So you play in a band?"

Katie cleared her throat and answered, "Yeah, I play fiddle in a band called Sterling. We're on Blake's tour for a couple of weeks."

"Sterling? Hey I think I've heard one of your songs. What's it called? 'Valentine'?" Luke leaned forward on his elbows, his blue eyes focused intently on Katie.

"That's right, it's 'Valentine'. Hopefully there will be more where that came from. We're planning on hitting the studio again after we're done with the tour."

"She's not just in the band, bro. She writes most of their lyrics too," Blake chimed in.

"Oh, so you're beautiful AND talented? No wonder Blake is so smitten," Roy teased.

"Y'all are embarrassing Katie. Now you leave her alone and let her eat her supper. Luke, what's new at work?" Betty steered the conversation away from Katie.

Katie wasn't embarrassed, she was intrigued. Blake was smitten? He had talked to his family about her? She tried to focus on Luke and his stories about the handsome pharmaceutical rep that had been visiting his office and making the nurses swoon, but her mind kept wandering to Blake. With his chair so close to hers, all she could think about was the way the warmth of his body reached hers, his spicy cologne, and the electricity that pulsed through her body when his hand brushed her skin.

She glanced at Blake and saw that his eyes were locked onto her. Katie blushed and purposefully turned towards Luke and forced herself to listen to the story. From the corner of her eye, she saw Betty smiling indulgently at Blake as she noticed her son's intense focus on Katie.

"Katie, I hope you saved room for dessert, hon. The banana pudding here is divine." Betty smiled at Katie as she motioned for the waitress.

"You've got to try the banana pudding, Katie; it's Betty Jackson's secret recipe. One bite, and you'll know why I never moved too far away from home," said Luke. Betty beamed at Luke, love and pride evident on her face.

"If it's anything like the pot roast, I'll have to make room, Mrs. Jackson. Everything has been delicious," said Katie.

"Now I'll have none of that. Mrs. Jackson is my mother-in-law. You call me Betty," insisted Betty.

"All right, Betty it is," said Katie shyly.

The waitress brought desserts for everyone and conversations halted once more as the group enjoyed dishes of banana pudding. Katie had never tasted anything so heavenly. Sitting at the table with such a loving family, basking in the warmth of Blake's affection, and eating the delicious dessert felt so perfect, so right, to Katie that tears sprang to her eyes. She blinked and looked away, hoping that nobody noticed.

Blake noticed, though, and leaned close to her. "Is everything all right?" he whispered into her ear.

Katie nodded, not trusting herself to speak. "Mmm hmm," she managed. She felt emotional, even wistful, and she wasn't sure why. The love she could feel between these four people was so warm, so complete. She took a deep breath and composed herself. "Everything is just so nice, and your family is great."

"Well, I think you're pretty great," said Blake before he planted an affectionate kiss on her temple.

"You're not so bad yourself," Katie breathed as she turned her head towards his.

"You ready to get out of here?" Blake whispered. His breath was hot on her ear and sent a shiver through Katie.

"Oh yeah," Katie managed.

"Well, as always, it was wonderful to see you, but Miss McCoy and I have to get going. We're kind of on a schedule," Blake announced to the table. He managed to look regretful and excited to leave at the same time.

"Honey, it sure was good to meet you. Blake has told us so much about you, and we are glad we got a chance to see you for ourselves," said Roy as he and Betty stood and made their way around the table. They each hugged Blake and Katie in turn, and Luke gave Blake a hearty hug, patted him on the back, and said his good-byes.

Luke turned to Katie and gave her a friendly hug. "I wasn't kidding about being single. If you have any friends half as pretty as you, send them my way," he teased.

"You're sweet to say that. I'll keep it in mind," Katie smiled at his compliment. "It sure was nice meeting y'all," Katie offered to the family as Blake took her hand and led her past tables of curious diners through the crowded restaurant.

They stepped out into the parking lot and scanned the rows of cars to find Blake's. He and Katie piled in and made their way through Knoxville back to the tour buses. Blake drove with one hand on the wheel and one hand on Katie's thigh, sending dizzying pings of electricity up and down her spine. The car's atmosphere was charged with the couple's awareness of each other. Katie found herself drawn closer to Blake's side of the car, and their eyes met as Blake slowed to a stop at a red light. Their gazes locked, Katie unbuckled her seat belt, and Blake pulled her head closer to him, closing the distance between them. He wound her hair around his fingers as their lips met. Katie placed a hand on the back of Blake's head and held him close as she deepened the kiss, her lips moving insistently against his. The moment stretched out like warm taffy, the kiss just as sweet.

The car behind them honked, and they pulled away from one another, the spell broken. They noticed that the light had turned green, and Blake chuckled and released his grip on Katie, then moved the car through the intersection. Katie grinned sheepishly and moved back to her side of the car, buckling herself back into her seat belt.

•••

They arrived at Blake's bus, and parked in the lot. "You want to come in?" Blake asked Katie.

"I do," she responded. Katie had a fleeting thought about what Blake might have in mind in the bus, alone with her, but quickly dismissed her fears. She would deal with each moment as it came.

Chapter Seven

Blake got out of the car and ran around to Katie's side to open her car door. "Shall we?" Blake led Katie to the door of his bus and invited her to walk ahead of him. Katie climbed the steps up to the bus's door with Blake close behind, admiring the view.

Blake joined her at the top of the steps and looked down at Katie, his blue eyes smoldering, and raised her hand to his lips. "Right this way," he said as he punched in the key code to the bus and pushed the door open.

Katie stepped in and gasped. She spun around to face Blake when he came in behind her. "Blake Jackson, this isn't a bus, this is an apartment on wheels! Actually, this is nicer than my apartment," she said with a laugh.

"So you like it?"

"Yeah, it's gorgeous. Show me around," said Katie as Blake took her hand again.

"Caroline actually did most of the decorating. I wanted it to feel like home, and it really needed a woman's touch." Blake explained.

Katie took in the plush taupe sofas and dark brown marble countertops in the front lounge area, the built-in desk holding a laptop that must belong to Caroline, the guitars hanging from wall-mounted brackets, a plasma screen television, and the glass door refrigerator stocked with a variety of drinks. She slipped out of her shoes and stepped onto a thick chocolate brown rug, sighing with pleasure. Blake led her through a hallway and pointed out a couple of guest bunks, a closed closet, and a guest bathroom.

Katie poked her head into the bathroom and gasped when she realized how much bigger and nicer Blake's guest bathroom was than the one her whole band shared. Blake showed her to a second lounge, easily twice the size of Sterling's, where there were inviting leather chairs, more guitars, framed photos of Blake with his family, yet another television screen, and a bar that housed a small refrigerator and baskets of snack foods. A pocket door separated the back lounge from what had to be Blake's bedroom. Katie wondered if she'd be invited to see that room too.

"So there you have it, home sweet home away from home," said Blake.

"I can't believe this place! It's gorgeous, and so much room for just one person. Unbelievable."

"Caroline rides with me a lot of the time, and sometimes I have some of the guys over. I'm on the road more than I'm at home, though, so this way I don't go crazy. I picked this bus a couple of years ago so I'd have enough room for two, you know, thinking ahead."

"For two?"

"I always imagined that I'd take my wife on the road with me and we'd see the country from this bus. You know, just the two of us, hitting the open road." Blake's blue eyes were intense. "I just haven't found my wife yet."

Blake led Katie through the pocket door and into his bedroom where a king-sized bed sat, a quilted chocolate brown bedspread turned down to reveal crisp ivory sheets, fluffy pillows lining the headboard, and a robin's egg blue knit blanket folded neatly at the foot. The air was cool and quiet; the low hum of the bus's air conditioning the only sound, and Katie could smell traces of Blake's spicy cologne in the air. Blake took Katie's hand, pulled her close to him, and enveloped her in a warm embrace.

"I'm glad you're here with me," he whispered, his voice husky with emotion. Blake pulled back and cupped Katie's face in his hands, captured her eyes with his gaze, and breathed, "God, you're gorgeous." He pressed his lips to hers, gently, as he ran his fingers through her hair. Katie responded and pulled him closer, deepening the kiss as her lips parted under his and his tongue explored her warm mouth. He tasted sweet, he smelled like home, and she never wanted the kiss to end. Katie's grip on Blake tightened as the kiss intensified, fireworks exploded in her head, and an electric energy passed between them.

Blake pulled Katie down onto his bed, his lips never leaving hers. They stretched out, side by side, and Blake explored her body, his hand moving from her shoulders down to the swell of her backside, to brush her thigh, and finally to tentatively cup her breast. She gasped but did not pull away, so he continued, squeezing gently and clearly enjoying the feel of her in his hand. He held her close to him, his other hand luxuriating in the feel of her silky hair winding around his fingers.

Blake moved until he was on top of Katie, propped on his elbows while she took his face in her hands and looked deep into his eyes before returning her lips to his. She shivered with pleasure when his lips trailed to her neck, his breath warm against her skin. Emboldened, Blake kissed her neck while his hand returned to her breast. Katie arched her body and a soft sound escaped her lips as she clutched his shoulders and held him close. He parted her legs with his knee and lowered his body onto hers, one hand working to unbutton her blouse as he propped himself up on his elbow.

"Blake," she whispered.

"Oh, Katie," he moaned.

"Blake." Katie's voice grew firm. He stilled and gazed down into her eyes, lust clouding his vision. "Blake, I'm so sorry but I can't do this."

"Oh, oh, okay, I'm sorry. I think I got carried away," he said as he moved off of her and stretched out beside her on the bed. Blake kissed her chastely on the forehead and inhaled deeply against the top of her head. Blake moved to get more comfortable on the bed, obviously trying to shift gears.

"No, I'm sorry, I should have said something before it got this far. I really like you, but I kind of promised myself to save sex for a serious commitment. I shouldn't have led you on; I guess I got carried away, too."

"Oh, I see. So you're like a…" He trailed off.

"Yes, I'm a virgin. It's kind of embarrassing, at my age, but it just hasn't happened for me yet. I've been so scared to tell you, scared to find out what you would think."

Blake cupped Katie's chin and gave her a soft kiss, then ran his hand over her hair. "It's certainly unusual, but I actually like that you've never been with anyone. It seems right for you."

She let out a relieved breath. "Thank you for saying that. I feel like such a baby about it sometimes, but it's become pretty important to me. When I was younger, I made the promise to myself that I would wait until I fell in love, and then with the band and everything that just never happened. The more committed I got to the band's success, the fewer boyfriends I had that were committed to me. Nobody has been able to handle it, and I don't want to compromise myself or my dreams for the kinds of guys I've come across."

"So you haven't found anyone who can understand what you're doing with the band?"

"Right, it's like when I meet someone they act like they think it's great that I'm in the band and we're getting so much work. When it comes down to it, though, nobody has been able to handle the time I have to spend rehearsing or playing gigs. Either that, or they're convinced that there's more going on between me and the guys than just work. I'm really sorry if I led you on, or if you aren't cool with my situation."

"Sweetheart, it's fine. Really. Whatever you're comfortable with is fine. I'll behave myself." Blake smiled down at her and kissed her softly.

"Thank you. This probably isn't what you're used to. I mean, getting shut down and all."

"Oh honey, you have no idea. I don't know what you think or what you've heard, but I spend most nights on tour alone. The only time I have a woman in this bus it's Caroline, and believe me, she is all business," he laughed. "I wasn't kidding when I said I haven't found my wife, and I don't think that sleeping around with anyone who shows up on the road is the best way to find her. It's damn near impossible to have anything real when I'm in a new town every other night."

Blake tucked his hands behind his head and eased back onto his bed. He turned to face Katie and said, "Being with you has been the most real thing I've had in a long time. That's probably why I've rushed you."

"You haven't rushed me," Katie said softly. "I've wanted everything that we've done to happen. I feel it too, you know, between us. It's scary for me though, how it's moving so fast. I haven't had a boyfriend or anything even close in a long time."

"I've been alone a long time too. There's not a lot of room for relationships in a career like this."

"I'll bet. I'm sure you get plenty of chances though, if you ever just want female attention." Katie smiled mischievously. "I doubt you'd have much trouble finding someone to share your bed in every town you visit."

"That might be true," Blake said, with a sly grin. "That's not what I want, though. I want someone to actually want to know me, know who I am. Most of the time I meet girls on the road and they want the picture with me, or they want to go back to tell their friends that we met. It's a strange situation, how everyone knows so much about me but nobody really knows me at all."

"Nobody? You know, I already feel like I know you, like I can trust you. It's just too bad we've got so little time together before I go back home."

"I've thought about that too, sweetheart. Maybe we can figure something out." Blake leaned over and kissed Katie's forehead. "Will you stay with me tonight? I promise to keep my hands to myself."

Katie giggled and kissed him. "I know you will. I trust you."

Blake pulled her close and inhaled deeply against her hair as his arms tightened around her. Katie felt her body respond to Blake's touch and pulled herself closer to him, and whispered, "All right," before surrendering to another deep kiss.

• • •

Katie grabbed her toothbrush and a fresh set of clothes to sleep in while Blake sat in the front lounge of Sterling's tour bus. Charles sat down on the sofa facing Blake and watched with amusement as the rest of Sterling tried to get ready for a night out in the cramped quarters.

"Looks like everyone's heading out tonight. It'll be good to get a little breathing room, I guess." Charles stretched his legs.

"You guys are already put-out with one another after only a few days on the road? Hopefully you'll find your rhythm before long."

"Mr. Jackson, it's not that we're put-out. It's just been a little stressful for everyone. We're not used to it, and we were already pretty cramped on board, so it will be nice to get a little breathing room. I'm a little disappointed that the reason we're getting it is because our Katie is going to your bus, though." Charles tried to sound casual, but the reproach in his voice was apparent.

"Well, Katie is an adult and can make her own decisions, but for what it's worth, I have real feelings for her and completely respect her. She's in good hands, Charles. There's no need to worry."

"I hope that's true. Katie is a sweet girl, and she's been through a lot. I'm just worried for her and don't want her falling for someone who will be gone and out of her life in less than two weeks." Charles sighed heavily and got up when Katie returned to the front lounge. "Y'all have a good night. We'll see you in the morning."

With that, Blake and Katie returned to his bus while the rest of Sterling piled into a cab to head out for a late night out. Everyone had publicity commitments during the day and a show tomorrow night, but they weren't about to pass up the chance to get out and see a new city. Nobody was on board the Sterling bus when a figure dressed all in black emerged from the parking lot's shadows and slashed the tires.

Chapter Eight

Soft sunlight streamed through the windows of Blake's bedroom and the insistent beep of his alarm clock nudged Katie from her sleep. She stretched, yawned, and a satisfied smile spread across her face as she remembered where she was. Blake was already awake, propped up on an elbow and watching Katie.

"Good morning, beautiful," Blake murmured as he ran the back of his hand gently down Katie's cheek. He kissed her forehead and asked, "How did you sleep?"

"Great. I can't remember the last time I slept so well."

"Me too," he said softly. "I think it's meant to be."

Katie giggled and pushed Blake's shoulder playfully. "I could get used to this, Mr. Jackson. Your bed is a lot nicer than my bunk. Your bus is a lot quieter than mine, too."

"Maybe you should just stay with me until you go home then," Blake said, suddenly serious.

Katie was stunned momentarily, not sure how to respond. On one hand, spending her days and nights with Blake sounded like a dream come true. She imagined ending each day on the tour snuggled up in his bed, cocooned together under the blankets, whispering together, and her heart squeezed with emotion. It would be so easy to trade in her tiny bunk on Sterling's tour bus for a spot next to the man of her dreams, blissfully passing the hours on the road in his arms instead of cramped in her little bed, pulling the curtain closed for any little scrap of privacy. Spending every night together might make it harder for her to keep her promise to herself, though. Katie couldn't imagine lying next to

Blake night after night, always remaining abstinent. Would it really be so bad if she did give in to her feelings for Blake? Or would it make it even harder to say goodbye when they went their separate ways?

Katie looked into Blake's dreamy blue eyes and melted against his warm, solid chest as he pulled her close and kissed her deeply. How could she ever say goodbye to him? A part of her realized that it was too soon to have feelings this strong for a man, it had to be. The constant togetherness and bubble of intimacy the tour provided intensified everything. Katie had already become accustomed to an 'us-against-the-world' mentality, finding herself feeling proprietary over Blake, like the only one who truly knew him.

"I'd love to spend every night with you, but I'll have to think—" Katie was cut off by loud rapping on the bus's door.

Blake groaned and pulled himself out of bed. He slid on a pair of shorts over his boxers and pulled a T-shirt over his head as he made his way to the front of the bus. He looked unbearably handsome, even rumpled and sleepy. Katie sat up and smoothed her hair, leaning over and craning her neck to see through the bedroom door. She couldn't see all the way to the front of the bus, but she heard Charles's voice when Blake let him in.

"We don't know exactly when it happened, but our tires were slashed last night. I called the police, but that's it. We didn't know if we should contact tour security or what exactly the protocol is for this kind of thing."

Katie hopped out of bed and hurried to the front. "The tires were slashed last night? Is everyone okay? Is anything else damaged? Did y'all see anybody?"

Charles looked down at Katie, his mouth set in a grim line. "We didn't see anybody. It was late when we got back to the bus last night, so we don't even know when it happened. It could've been done while we were away or it could've happened while we were sleeping. We didn't see anything or notice it when we got back and we never saw or heard anything when we were on board last night. There's no other damage or sign of trouble."

Blake picked up his phone and dialed, then wandered to the back lounge as he spoke with tour security.

Katie sat down on a sofa, shaking with fear and anger. "Who would do such a thing? Some crazed jealous fan?"

"It could be some random crime, could be somebody with mental illness, we just don't know. Could be personal, you know, you hear about fans who think they have a connection to a celebrity. Honestly we're surprised it was our bus and not Blake's. That's what's really confusing. Hopefully the police will be able to find some evidence. I'm sure that Blake will get security tightened up and you'll be safe while we figure everything out." Charles sat beside Katie and rubbed her back. "It's going to be all right, kiddo. I promise."

Katie put her head in her hands while tears streamed down her face. She looked up into Charles's kind eyes and cried, "God, what if it's some crazy person obsessed with Blake? What if they're trying to get rid of me?"

"I don't know, sweetheart, but it's going to be fine. I really don't think you should read that much into it before we know what happened. Chances are it was just a random act of vandalism, maybe some prank." Charles continued to rub Katie's back and tried to soothe her.

Blake returned to the front lounge and set his phone down on Caroline's desk. "Security is on their way. They'll meet with the police and then they'll probably want to talk with you guys. I want Katie to stay with me while they check everything out. I can ask Caroline to help find a place to get the tires replaced while we're on site today. We'll probably have to get a few extra guys out to watch over the buses while we're away, too. The drivers will be here but they shouldn't have to worry about this while they are getting the rigs ready to roll out."

Katie began crying again in earnest. Blake sat down beside her and pulled her close, holding her in his arms. Charles stood up and awkwardly moved towards the door, not sure whether to stay or go. Blake stroked Katie's hair and kissed her tear-streaked cheeks while he whispered to her softly. He looked up and met Charles's eyes and waved him out. "I've got her. You go on ahead."

Katie took a deep breath and wiped her tears away with the back of her hand. "I'm scared, Blake. I feel like this is because of me."

"Hey, look at me." Blake's voice was firm but gentle, and Katie turned her tear-stained face towards him. "This is NOT your fault, sweetheart. I don't want to hear that again," he insisted. "There's no reason to think that this happened because of you or that you're in any danger. We'll get extra security out here until we find out what happened."

"I just feel horrible. I don't know how we're going to afford this, and we were barely starting to break even as it was, between the tour and all our new expenses. You know? Now we're going to need new tires, more security, and that means more money. The guys aren't going to come out and say it, but they've got to think it's because of me. I don't know what to do," she finished weakly.

"You're not a liability, and I don't know why on earth you think that this is somehow your fault. Even if this is the work of a fan trying to send a message to you, it's still not your fault. I'm sure insurance will cover the tires and if not, it's just money. I can pay for the tires, and I'm happy to do it. Nobody thinks this is your fault. The guys really care about you, you know, I can tell when I see y'all together. All you need to worry about right now is staying safe and doing your job. We'll figure the rest out." Blake planted a kiss on Katie's forehead and smoothed a lock of hair behind her ear.

Just being near Blake, safe in his arms soothed Katie. His confidence almost made her believe that everything would turn out all right. Katie was humbled by Blake's unconditional promise to keep her safe, by his offers to care for her without hesitation. She could fall in love with this man. It would be so easy. And it was going to be so hard to let him go.

• • •

Blake sat in the front lounge of his massive tour bus, across the desk from Caroline Mathers. She looked at him over the top of her glasses and crossed her legs under her chair as she leaned forward on her elbows.

"So let me get this straight, you want to hire a security guard just for Katie, and you haven't asked her what she thinks?"

"That's exactly what I want, Caro. Until we get the buses checked out, until we have an idea of what we're dealing with here, I don't feel comfortable having her exposed to danger. I can't stay with her myself, so this is the only way we can be sure she's okay. I don't think I'll be able to concentrate any other way."

"Do you want to pull someone from the security detail or find an outside firm? You don't think there's some kind of conspiracy or inside job, do you?" Caroline bit her lip and looked like she was trying to disguise her amusement.

"I'm a reasonable man," Blake said with a laugh, his eyes dancing. "If we have someone on staff already who we can pull for Katie, that would be fine."

"I'll go check with the head of security and see if someone can be spared for the special Katie McCoy security detail." She smiled indulgently. "Do you want to tell her yourself?"

"I'll call her if you can find someone for her. And stop laughing at me, this is serious." Blake balled up a piece of paper and tossed it at Caroline.

She deflected the paper. "I know, I know, this is important. I'm just not used to this side of you. I've never seen you care for someone like this, and I've certainly never seen you so protective of anyone before. Katie must be a very special girl."

"She really is."

Blake picked up his phone to call Katie and Caroline left to meet with the head of security.

• • •

Katie put thoughts of the bus and the police out of her mind as she tried to relax in her dressing room before the show. Her hair and makeup team was hard at work transforming her for the night, and they seemed to sense that Katie wasn't in a chatty mood. They worked quietly as Katie took deep breaths and willed herself to focus on the show and forget about the negative energy surrounding her. There was extra security at the buses, and they hadn't heard about any trouble since the morning. Katie was as safe as she was going to get and there was nothing more anyone could do right now. The vandal had ruined her morning, no use in letting him—or her—ruin her band's show tonight, too.

Caroline knocked on her dressing room door and poked her head inside. "Ms. McCoy? I know you're busy getting ready, but I just need to quickly introduce you to your new security guard. Do you have a moment?"

"Sure, come on in," Katie answered.

Caroline breezed into Katie's dressing room on a cloud of subtle perfume and competency, her expensive-looking high heels clacking on the concrete floor. An imposing, handsome blond man dressed in a perfectly pressed charcoal grey suit stood behind her, stoic and serious behind wire frame glasses. He looked vaguely familiar to Katie and she tried to place him, coming up short until

Cara and Tiffany started giggling. He was the gorgeous security guard they had been swooning over a couple of days ago.

"Did Mr. Jackson speak with you already about how you would have your own security until the vandalism problem is cleared up?" Caroline asked.

Katie nodded and Caroline continued. "This is Jonathan James and he's been assigned to you. He will just be watching over you and making sure that any threats against you are contained. We'd like to ask you to exercise caution, you know, be a little more aware of your surroundings and let Jonathan know immediately if you notice anything out of the ordinary."

"I will, but having a personal bodyguard seems a little extreme." Katie managed a nervous smile.

"I'm sure it's overkill, but Mr. Jackson feels very strongly about making sure that you are safe. Feel free to call me if you have any questions."

With that, Caroline left Jonathan alone with Katie, Cara, and Tiffany, her footsteps fading as she made her way through the venue.

"So, should I call you Jonathan or Mr. James?" Katie gave the serious man a winsome smile.

"Jonathan is fine, ma'am. We'll be spending a lot of time together so please feel free to get comfortable. I'm going to try to stay out of your way for the most part. I'm just here to make sure nothing happens to you, so try to forget I'm around if you can."

Tiffany and Cara stifled giggles and Katie laughed. "Well I don't know if we can forget you're here but we'll do our best."

Jonathan surprised them with a quick grin that revealed very white, very straight teeth. "All right, ladies, then if you don't need anything I'll step outside. I'll be right outside your door."

Jonathan stepped aside as Blake came in and poked his head in the door. "Can I come in?" He gave Katie an irresistible boyish smile.

"Sure, come on in, we're all decent in here," Katie responded. She slid off her chair and smiled in anticipation. Seeing Blake was exactly what she needed.

Blake made his way into the dressing room, oblivious to the charged energy that filled the space when he entered. The hair and makeup girls were frozen in place, and Katie realized that they had probably never met him. "Come on in. We're just doing hair and makeup. This is my dream team, Tiffany and Cara. Girls, this is Blake."

Blake crossed the room and shook each girl's hand in turn. "It's nice to meet you, ladies. I think you've got your work cut out for you; it's hard to improve on perfection." He laughed good-naturedly and the women giggled. Blake kissed Katie gently and squeezed her hand. "I just wanted to check in on you. Caroline said that there had been no sign of trouble today, and I see that you met Jonathan. Is everything all right?"

"Everything is fine. It's a little weird to have a muscled bodyguard standing outside my door but I'm managing. I'm just trying to relax and focus on the show." Katie tried to ignore the curious stares of Tiffany and Cara. "Jonathan seems like he'll take good care of me, and I'm doing all right."

Blake pulled Katie closer and kissed the top of her head. "All right, that's good. I've got an interview to get to before the show, so if you need anything just ask Jonathan or Caroline. If there's an emergency, get them to pull me away. Please just make sure you're close to Jonathan until I can get back to you. I know that you're in good hands, but I won't feel comfortable until you're back in mine."

"I'll be fine. Don't worry about me; I'll see you tonight."

Blake reluctantly released his hold on Katie, pressed another warm, lingering kiss on her lips, and left her dressing room. Katie sat back down in her chair and sighed contentedly as she watched him leave. The view was just as good coming as going. Katie laughed when she realized that Tiffany and Cara hadn't moved an inch from where they stood when they met Blake. The girls stood perfectly still, mouths agape, staring at Katie. She cleared her throat and they snapped back to attention.

"Oh. My. God. You and Blake Jackson are together? He is so hot!" Tiffany squealed. She rooted around in her bag and found a blush brush.

"He really is gorgeous. Like seriously, the best looking guy I've ever seen. He even smells good," Cara said as she practically swooned.

"He is pretty amazing," Katie admitted. "I am one lucky girl."

"Lucky? It's like you won the boyfriend lottery, honey. That man is sex on two legs." Tiffany laughed as she swirled the brush in Katie's blush and swept it across Katie's cheeks.

Katie giggled. "I'll tell him you think so."

"You'll do no such thing!" Tiffany flushed with embarrassment. "I can make you look like a clown, missy."

Katie threw up her hands in surrender. "Okay, Okay, not a word," she promised with a laugh.

"He's, like, an amazing kisser, isn't he? You can tell by just looking at him." Cara asked Katie with a dreamy look on her face.

Katie hugged herself and gave the girls a conspiratorial smile. "Yeah, it's pretty amazing. I mean, he is a really good kisser. Sometimes I feel like it's got to be a dream. Like there's no way this could be happening to me."

"Well, I'm totally jealous, girl. That man is beautiful." Cara said.

Tiffany and Cara finished Katie's hair and makeup, and Jonathan accompanied Katie to her band's pre-show meeting. Once she left the safe haven of her dressing room, she felt exposed and her nerves were frazzled, but she forced herself to put herself in the hands of the security team and focus on the show. It was a relief knowing that once they finished the Knoxville show that the bands would load into their buses and head out for Nashville. Of course, someone could just as easily follow them to the next city, but at least for tonight she could relax on the bus, confident that no one would be able to reach them.

• • •

The buses rolled into Nashville in the early morning hours while the musicians slept. Once they woke up, the day would be full of press and fan events before the show. Blake Jackson was Nashville's pride and joy, and since word had gotten out about his romance with the gorgeous young fiddler in the opening act, everybody wanted a piece of the story. Katie and her new bodyguard Jonathan were both on board Blake's bus, as the police found no evidence on or around his bus after the tires were slashed on hers. There were no fingerprints, no usable footprints, nobody saw anything, and nothing was left behind.

On board Blake's bus, Katie awoke to the annoying beep of the alarm and the tempting aroma of coffee brewing in the kitchen. Jonathan was already up and working on his laptop at Caroline's desk. She could hear the clack of his keyboard as he worked, probably checking the morning news and catching up on emails. She stretched and luxuriated in the feel of Blake's expensive sheets and his soft mattress. Every moment she spent on Blake's bus reminded her of how much shabbier her own was. She loved being with her band and was proud of all that they had accomplished, but Blake's bus sure was nice. He slept beside her, his long lashes dark against his gorgeous face. She could stare at him all day. His tousled hair and faint stubble made him seem more vulnerable to her. So different from the man who filled a room with his presence, who handled every problem that came their way with authority, who had kept her safe from harm. Katie's eyes felt hot as tears threatened to fall as she gazed at this beautiful man. This beautiful man who would be out of her life in just a few days. How was she going to say goodbye? How could she forget him?

She slid out of bed, careful not to wake Blake, and pulled on a pair of shorts. She had slept in Blake's T-shirt and loved that it smelled like him. Katie planned to keep it on as long as she could, thought she might just pack it in her bags and take it home with her. She padded down the hallway to the front lounge where Jonathan was seated at Caroline's desk, eyes focused on the laptop screen. "I made coffee," he said without looking up. He was already dressed in a charcoal custom-tailored suit and looked alert and ready for the day.

"Thanks," she murmured as she poured a cup and doctored it with cream and sugar. "Anything happening?"

She sat down on one of the leather sofas and blew on the steaming cup in her hands. Jonathan peered at Katie over wire-rimmed glasses, looking handsome and very serious. "Nothing has been reported. Now we're working with event staff and local law enforcement to secure the area as well as we can. Nashville is especially problematic due to the high volume of fans and press. We've called in some reinforcements and we're trying to figure out the logistics so that everyone's safety is a top priority without affecting the flow of the day. Most of it has very little to do with the vandalism incident, because the fan base here is so large compared to other areas. We are just taking a few extra precautions now that we know that there is a chance that our perpetrator may have followed us into town. Mr. Jackson has a lot on his schedule today and it is imperative that nothing is left to chance in all the activity."

"Yeah he's from here and they love him. I'm sure it's going to be a madhouse. He promised a lot of time to fan events and press stuff today and I know he doesn't want to miss anything," Katie said. She took a sip of her coffee. "You make excellent coffee, Jonathan."

"I used to work at Starbucks."

"Really? I'm trying to picture you in a green apron, cleaning out those big machines, handing out banana bread."

"No, not really," he deadpanned, then grinned. His sense of humor caught Katie off guard. She could definitely see why the other girls were so interested in Jonathan.

"You're pretty funny for a bodyguard, you know."

Blake ambled into the front lounge, stretched, and smiled at Katie with sleepy eyes. He was so good-looking in his rumpled state that Katie had to remind herself to breathe. "Good morning, gorgeous. You sleep well?"

"I did, thank you. Jonathan made coffee."

Blake poured himself a cup of coffee and sat down by Katie on the sofa. He nodded to Jonathan. "Good morning. Any new developments?" He sipped his coffee. "This is some damn good coffee."

Katie giggled and tucked her feet under her as she curled up next to Blake, happily accepting the kiss he planted on her forehead. Jonathan responded. "No sir, there have been no signs of trouble since we arrived and everything appears to be going according to plan. We're working to develop today's security plan in order to maximize our effectiveness without hindering your day's activities. I understand that Nashville is one of your most important stops?"

"Yeah, this is my hometown, so I always try to fit in as much as I can when we roll in. It's going to be a busy day, so we should go ahead and get started. I've got to meet with Caroline on site as soon as I get a shower. I know I have a lot on my plate today, but I'm not sure what you guys are doing for Sterling. If you have Miss McCoy's schedule, I'll trust you to get her where she needs to be." Blake kissed Katie and added, "I don't know how much we'll see each other today, babe. Try to have a good time and stay safe."

"I've got everything we need," said Jonathan, holding up a printed itinerary. "I'll accompany Miss McCoy back to the

Sterling bus and I will be with her on site as well. Don't worry about a thing."

"Great. Well, darlin', I will see you whenever I can. Have a good day." Blake pulled Katie close and planted a gentle kiss on her lips, lingering a bit before reluctantly releasing her and standing up. He took his coffee and his phone and headed towards the back of the bus while Katie and Jonathan left to meet the rest of her band.

• • •

Blake settled back onto a couch in his dressing room and flashed his signature smile at the young reporter sent to interview him for a Nashville magazine. The pretty young redhead was the fourth journalist to interview Blake today, but he gave her the same enthusiasm he gave the last three interviewers. She started with the typical questions about the latest album, the tour, his influences, and life on the road. Blake gave her the typical answers. She took her glasses off and looked at Blake intently. "Mr. Jackson, rumor has it that you've been spending a lot of time with a special lady. Care to comment?"

"Rebecca, is it?" The journalist nodded. "Rebecca, I try to keep my personal life very private, but I like you. I'll just say this. There is someone very special to me, someone that I have come to care for very much. I love spending time with her, and we have a lot of fun together."

Rebecca grinned. "Thanks for the scoop. Will you share her name?"

Blake smiled slyly at the young reporter. "Let's just say that she's a talented musician, a gifted songwriter, and a knockout Texas beauty." He checked his watch. "I'm sorry, darlin', but I think our time is up. It was nice talking with you."

Caroline Mathers ushered the reporter out and sat back down at the table in Blake's dressing room. She listened to a voicemail and began checking emails on her BlackBerry while Blake got a cold drink out of the tub on a counter and returned to the couch to push his boots off his feet.

"All right, Caro. What's up next?" Blake took a sip of his drink.

"We have a radio station fan event for you in about an hour, and then that's it. You'll be free to relax until your show."

"How's everything looking with Katie? Any problems or anything?"

"Actually, I just received a brief from Jonathan and so far it looks like everything is fine. There's been no sign of anything unusual or any trouble today." Caroline pulled a paper out of a folder. "We received this picture from the security film the night the tires were slashed." She passed a picture to Blake.

"You can't see anything here," he said. The photo showed a shadowy figure dressed in black as he or she approached the bus. The perpetrator wore black pants, a black shirt, and a black knitted cap covered his or her head. "I can't even tell if this is a man or a woman." He tossed the picture to the table in frustration. They didn't even know who they were watching out for.

Chapter Nine

Katie sat in a row of folding chairs with the rest of her band and squirmed uncomfortably. Sterling was doing a radio interview, and after a couple of perfunctory questions addressed to the whole band about their album and future plans, the DJ had focused all his attention on Katie.

"You're quite a bit younger than the rest of the band, aren't you?" The DJ, Steve Norris, asked Katie.

"Yes, but we are a great team. The guys were together for quite a while before we met, and they welcomed me into the family."

"So things really took off for Sterling once you joined the band?"

"I wouldn't say that. We played small gigs and struggled just like any band for a couple of years after I joined. I have been with them since I was eighteen and it's been six years. I'd hardly say that my addition to the lineup was a major catalyst."

"Sure, sure. I just mean that nobody had ever heard of Sterling before they got a young beautiful fiddler. I'm sure that doesn't hurt." Steve smiled at the band. "And here you are now, touring with the country's biggest star. How has that been?"

"We have really enjoyed being on the road with Blake Jackson, and the fans have been incredible. We've been having a great time, and Mr. Jackson has treated us very well." Charles Cranston answered, jumping in before the DJ could ask another question of Katie.

"I hear that Mr. Jackson is treating one of you *very* well, if you know what I mean. Rumor has it that Mr. Jackson has taken a special liking to Katie. Care to comment?"

"You'll have to ask Blake about that, I'm afraid. We'd love to talk about the tour or our album, though." Katie hoped the DJ would take the hint and focus on the band.

"I think I have everything I need. You guys have a great show tonight, thanks!" Steve wrapped up the interview as radio staff members gathered the equipment. "Can I get a photo with you?"

Sterling posed for a photo with the Nashville DJ and then returned to their dressing rooms to get ready for the show. Tension strummed between them as they made their way through the venue's hallways. Katie stopped suddenly.

"Guys, I'm sorry about the interview. If there were a way to get everyone to focus on the band and leave me out of it, I would love that. Believe me; I don't want any extra attention."

"We know, Katie. We're all just worn out from the travel and everyone could use some rest. It's hard on everyone." Jeff, Sterling's guitar player, looked at her kindly.

"Let's take a break and meet up for the pre-show," Katie offered.

"All right, that sounds great. We'll see you later, kiddo," Jeff agreed, maybe a little too quickly.

Jonathan led Katie to her dressing room and the rest of the band went in the opposite direction down another hall towards theirs. She watched the guys walk down the hall, away from her, and her heart squeezed with affection for them. They had done so much for her since she joined the band. They all had years more experience than her, but had never made her feel like she was any less a professional than any of them. They had shown her the ropes, had taught her everything she needed to know about the music business. They had even helped her parents feel more comfortable about letting her go out on the road. She was technically an adult at eighteen when she joined the band, but of course her parents would always see her as their little girl. The guys were so reliable and protective of her that her parents were soon just as comfortable as she was with them. They were the ones who helped her develop her stage presence, who taught her the tricks of staying sane on the road, and kept her believing in their success when things looked bleak.

She could tell that they were less than thrilled with the individual attention she had been getting in the press. They had always presented themselves as a cohesive unit in the past, so she wasn't exactly comfortable with it herself. They had never been in the national spotlight before either, though, so a lot had changed. She couldn't help that she had fallen for Blake, and she certainly couldn't help that people loved the story. Was she supposed to forgo any relationships outside the band so that the guys didn't get jealous? She'd had enough of jealous men to last her a lifetime. It wasn't her fault that the media was focused on her, not only as the lone young female in a group of older men but also as the love interest of Blake Jackson. They hadn't said a word to her about it, but she could see it on their faces and hoped that they would understand, or at least not resent her for everything.

Katie and Jonathan reached her dressing room and she looked forward to a quiet hour of rest before her hair and makeup team arrived. Blake was doing interviews all afternoon and she was on her own for a while. Jonathan checked his BlackBerry and did a quick security sweep of her dressing room while she settled down onto her couch. She checked her phone and saw that Blake had left her a voicemail. She smiled giddily and pressed the phone to her ear, so happy that just a message from him could have this effect on her. His deep sexy voice came through the line and sent a thrill through her.

"Hi sweetheart, it's me. Hope you're having a great day. I know mine will be a lot better when you're in my arms again. Listen, we don't have to roll out until pretty late tomorrow, so I was wondering if you'd like to take a little drive tomorrow afternoon after my last event to see my house here. I'll make sure that there's food in the kitchen and I'll cook for you. Call me when you get this."

Katie grinned up at Jonathan, who was finishing his inspection. "Blake invited me to his house here in town. He's even going to cook, how adorable is that?" She sighed and dropped her head back against the sofa.

"He's ever so dreamy," Jonathan teased, flashing Katie a grin.

"You know he is! Don't you have some bad guys to watch out for or something?" She tossed a throw pillow at him playfully as he headed for the door. When she was alone, Katie picked her phone up to call Blake.

Blake answered after several rings, and Katie could hear voices in the background. "Hello?" She could hear the smile in his voice.

"Hey, got your message. Is this a bad time?"

"No, Katie, this is a great time." Blake answered, and then Katie heard chatter and whistles erupt in the background.

"What's going on?" Katie said suspiciously.

"Nothing, darlin', just chatting with the press and a small group of fans." A cheer went up in the background.

"Seriously? You should have let me go to voicemail then. You're obviously busy."

"Never too busy for you, babe," Blake responded.

"You are too much, Blake Jackson. I just wanted to let you know that I'd love to see your house. Can you even cook?"

"I've got my mama's recipes, and you know how good those are," Blake said.

"That's true. All right, come see me when you can. Get back to work." Katie hung up with a laugh, shaking her head at the adorable Blake Jackson.

• • •

Blake met Katie at her bus after the bands were packed up for the drive into Memphis. Sterling had enjoyed a full day of press and fan events, and Katie had been relieved that the tension she had perceived the day before had been absent. No reporters focused on Katie or on her romance with Blake. Everyone was in high spirits and ready to enjoy a night out in Nashville. If she hadn't been looking forward to a nice long date with Blake, Katie might have been disappointed to miss out on spending time with her band.

"You ready to hit the road, darlin'?" He gestured to a shiny black extended cab pickup in the parking lot. He squinted into the sunlight, and Katie took the hand that he offered.

"I'm ready. 'Bye guys, y'all be careful out there." Katie waved to her band mates and let Blake lead her across the parking lot to the pickup.

"Did y'all have a good day?" Blake asked. He opened her door and helped her up into the truck.

"We really did. Nashville is such a great town. The people were awesome, and everything is so nice. I can't wait to see your house." Katie answered.

Blake hurried around and hopped into the driver's seat. "I love when I get to drive myself for a change." He grinned at her and started the engine. Blake turned the radio down as he pulled out of the parking lot, and he and Katie kept up a steady stream of conversation as they drove through town to Blake's Nashville home.

Blake eventually pulled into the driveway of a big flagstone house that reminded Katie of a fancy hunting lodge. Bright landscape lighting flooded across a beautifully manicured emerald green lawn and big flat stones dotted the lawn in a winding walkway up to the front porch which boasted beautifully tended potted plants, an inviting cushioned porch swing, and a pair of rocking chairs. Someone gone as often as Blake couldn't have a dog, but she halfway expected to see a big golden retriever bound up to meet them when they parked.

"Want me to show you around, or are you starving?" Blake asked as he helped Katie down from the truck.

"Show me around while it's still light out." She hopped down and took Blake's hand. She loved the warmth of his hand, how his skin felt rough next to hers, and how small and feminine she felt next to him.

Blake led Katie around back, where she saw a huge covered patio boasting what looked like a full outdoor kitchen, dining table, and plenty of chairs. She wondered if Blake was home enough to entertain or if all this went to waste. There was enough room for several dozen people to mingle comfortably. A fire pit caught her attention, and she pictured cuddling up under a warm blanket and roasting marshmallows outside when it finally got colder. It was hard to believe that she would be gone and out of Blake's life soon when it was so easy to picture herself sitting out here with him sharing secrets and kisses under the stars.

They wandered down a flagstone path through thick, dark green, well-tended grass towards a big barn. Blake led Katie inside and she inhaled the scent of cut grass, gasoline, and wood. Tools of every kind lined the shelves of a wall of tool benches, lawn maintenance equipment sat in a neat row along another wall, and a battery-powered radio sat atop a shelf below an old aluminum feed store sign. Blake clicked it on and Willie Nelson's familiar voice filled the barn.

"Darlin'?" Blake held out his hands to Katie, inviting her to dance. She joined him, and knew that she would never forget a single detail of the moment. She could feel the warmth of his skin through her clothes, could feel his faint stubble on her forehead and pulling lightly in her hair. His voice was low, deep, and husky as he sang along with the radio.

Katie pulled back enough to look up at Blake, and swallowed the urge to cry. Being in his arms felt like she had come home, like she had found a part of her that she hadn't even realized was missing. The end of the tour would come too quickly, and Katie couldn't imagine a future without Blake in it. She rested her head on Blake's shoulder and he kissed the top of her head.

She snuggled closer and sighed. "I'm going to miss you."

"Me, too, sweetheart, but let's not get into that right now. I'd like to concentrate on having a nice night together instead of getting depressed about what's to come." Blake pulled her closer, wrapping her in his arms. He breathed in the scent of her hair as if trying to memorize her.

He led her out of the barn and back across the lawn. It was beginning to get dark as afternoon slipped into evening, crickets were chirping, and the landscape lighting was coming on as they rounded the corner and stepped up onto the wraparound porch out front. Blake unlocked the door and invited Katie inside the house. She stepped in and gasped as she took in the gorgeous rustic interior of his home. The whole place looked like it had been torn from the pages of a magazine. Blake had chosen natural stone flooring and customized lighting for the foyer. French doors led to a dimly lit library, hand-scraped wood floors, oversized brown leather chairs, and built-in bookcases full to bursting with beautifully bound books gave the room an elegant but welcoming feel. He led her into the living area, where she passed sumptuous-looking leather furniture, a natural stone fireplace, more built-in bookcases, and a giant flat screen television. They made their way into Blake's gourmet kitchen, past the dining table that could comfortably seat twelve, and Katie took in his state of the art appliances, the gorgeous granite countertops, and the beautiful fixtures. The kitchen looked like it could be featured in a decorating magazine, but it somehow still seemed like a real home. Blake had nice things, but they all appeared to have been used. Nothing was there just for show.

She noticed framed family photographs lining a counter. She smiled at an image of Betty and Roy looking into each other's eyes and beaming. She noticed a picture of an elated Luke wearing a cap and gown, arms linked with a proud-looking Blake. He led Katie to a barstool and invited her to sit and have a drink while he disappeared into his walk-in pantry. He emerged with an armful of supplies and set them on his oversized kitchen island. He rummaged through his refrigerator for the rest of his ingredients and put everything on the island before turning on a stereo that Katie hadn't seen before. Soft music filled the space, and Katie sat, mesmerized, while Blake washed, chopped, and mixed ingredients. He was at home in the kitchen. Katie could imagine him cooking big meals at his mother's side, and wondered if that was how he learned to cook. Blake chopped up russet potatoes and then set them to boil on the impressive Viking stove top, seasoned some pork chops, and put together a beautiful green salad while Katie sipped on iced tea.

"Hope you're hungry," he said, looking up at Katie with a smile.

"Mmm hmm. Everything looks amazing. I can't remember the last time someone made a meal for me."

"You deserve a nice meal, sweetheart. I wish we could do it more often. I was hoping that we could take the four wheelers out and go for a ride, you know, get a little mud on the tires, but I'm afraid it's too dark. I'm working on getting lighting put up out on the property, but for now it's a little dangerous unless you know your way around. I'm afraid you'd tip yourself over or get lost out on the trails. Maybe next time we can come out earlier or I'll have lights up."

"Sounds like fun. I didn't notice a trail, just trees, trees, and more trees."

"Just a little ways out back, there's a big barn. Once you get out there, there are a couple of trails winding down through the woods through to the back of the property. It's hard to picture at night, but it's beautiful out there. Nothing but nature as far as you can see. No neighbors, no street noise, nothing but wind through the branches and birds in the trees. There's nothing like it. Whenever I get off a long stretch of travel and get out there, sometimes it's even too quiet at first. I get too used to the road noise and all the people on tour."

"Wow, well, I hope I get to see it some time." Katie was suddenly shy. Once they left his house tonight, the bands would hit the road and head to Memphis. After the Memphis show, there were only four days left on tour and Katie would be on her way back to Texas. Did Blake think that they would still be together in several months? Was this just small talk?

Katie looked into the living room and imagined cuddling up with Blake on the couch, having cozy conversations or watching television. She saw the screened-in porch just outside the dining room and pictured herself inviting friends over for lemonade or just sitting out there in a rocking chair watching a couple of dogs run around the backyard. Blake's home was amazing, but it was homey enough for her to feel like she could belong there. She imagined pictures of her and Blake joining the family pictures lining the counter. Katie shook her head, clearing the fantasy from her mind. She couldn't invite friends over for lemonade and girl talk. She didn't know anybody in Nashville and she had no reason to think that this wouldn't be her last visit to Blake's home. It made her heart hurt just to think about it, but it was likely that this time next year she would be nothing more than a memory for Blake.

Blake assembled plates of food for them and set them on the bar in front of Katie. "I'll grab forks and napkins if you'll take the plates to the table. Supper's ready." Katie took two plates to the table while Blake bundled up forks and napkins and carried two glasses of iced tea.

Katie sat down and tucked into her dinner. She let out a contented sigh after her first bite of the perfectly seasoned pork chop. "This is delicious. You are a man of many talents."

"Thank you, darlin'. It's my mama's recipe. She taught me everything I know about cooking."

"This is so much better than eating on the bus." Katie laughed before taking another bite and savoring her food.

"I wanted you to have a couple of weeks of venue catering as your sole source of nutrition before cooking for you. Makes mine taste better."

"Well, it certainly worked. I could definitely get used to this."

Katie took a sip of her iced tea and watched Blake with affection as he speared a bite of salad with his fork. What a gorgeous man. Tall, dark, and handsome, firm muscles, soft touchable waves of dark hair, dreamy blue eyes you could lose yourself in, those beautiful kissable lips. How was she ever going to forget him? If only he had been nothing more than a delicious piece of eye candy, maybe she could forget him then. Unfortunately, he also happened to be talented, funny, and incredibly caring. And sexy. Incredibly sexy.

Blake put down his fork and settled his gaze on Katie. "Katie, I'm fixin' to ask you something and I want you to think about it. You don't have to answer right away, or even tonight."

"Okay, what is it?" Katie's nerves jangled with anticipation. Why was he suddenly so serious?

"All right, here goes. I have had the best time with you the last couple of weeks, and I'm not ready for things to end. I don't know if you feel the same way, but I'm really falling for you. I don't want to freak you out by moving too fast, but I want to see what we have together. It seems strange, I know, but being on tour makes things different. We only have a few more days left before y'all are supposed to head back to Texas, and I don't think that's enough. I want you to stay." Blake looked into Katie's eyes intensely, took her hand in his and squeezed. "With me."

"What do you mean? You want to sign Sterling on for more shows?" Confusion and restrained excitement swirled together within her.

"Well, no. We already have the opening bands lined up for the rest of the tour. I was thinking that when the rest of the band goes home, you might stay with me. We could be together." Blake shifted uncomfortably in his chair, the look of anticipation fading from his face.

"You mean, like, you want me to go with you on your tour? On your bus? Just to go? To tag along?"

"I don't really mean it that way, you know, ah, I just thought we could spend more time together if you stayed with me. We can get to know each other, you know? See the country together. I thought it would be fun," he finished weakly.

"Sterling is supposed to go back into the studio when we're off this tour. We have new material to record, and we want to build on the momentum we've gained from being on this tour. We have gigs lined up in Austin after this. If I don't go back home, I'm pretty sure they'll replace me. They won't just wait to see if I come back."

"Well, maybe we can talk to the guys."

"Talk to them? You mean you want me to ask them to put their careers, their dreams, on hold while I take a little vacation?" Katie's heard her voice take on an angry quality but couldn't stop herself.

"I don't know. All I know is that I don't want you to go home and I have to keep going. The tour won't stop, and I don't know what will happen to you and me if we go our separate ways. I am sorry that I didn't think about what Sterling is going to do after this, I didn't think it through. I just want you with me."

"So you pretty much just thought about yourself, huh?"

"Don't be like that. I'm asking you to stay with me. I'm sitting here, telling you that I want to be with you, and you're making me out to be some kind of selfish jerk."

Blake was so surprised that she hadn't agreed immediately. Katie didn't know if she felt sorry for him or if she was infuriated. As much as she wanted to spend all of her days with Blake, she didn't imagine that she'd have to give up her career, her livelihood, to do so. Did he really want her to stay with him that badly? Or was he used to people putting their needs aside whenever he asked? Did he think she should brush her career to the side without a thought? Did he think she should travel the country on a bus with him just to see if they had something special? With him, when he had made no commitment to her? What did he imagine she would do if things didn't work out between them when she had no band or career to return home to?

Blake Jackson was a caring, sensitive man, but he was a man who was used to getting what he wanted, when he wanted it. He was also apparently a man who was used to putting himself first. This discussion made it crystal clear to Katie that Blake hadn't ever had to really consider anyone else. He was a successful man, a giant in his field, but maybe he had come to take his fame for granted. It had been years since he had been at Katie's level, in the first stages of success, looking forward to a bright future. He must have forgotten what it felt like to want success, to be so close to making it that you could taste it.

"I want to be with you. I really do. But I don't know if I am ready or willing to give up on my dreams to do it. I won't ask the band to wait for me, and I don't want to leave them just to see what might happen between you and me. If we had a solid commitment to one another, that might be different. But we haven't made any promises to each other. I have always wanted to be a musician, and I want to be successful more than almost anything. Almost anything. The only thing I want more is love. I want true, knock your socks off, once in a lifetime, love. I want that more than anything." Tears welled in Katie's eyes and threatened to spill over her lashes. "I know it's soon, probably too soon, but if you could tell me that you think that's what we have, that you do love me, then I will stay. Even if you just think that you might love me, then that's enough. But you have to tell me. You have to say the words."

Blake looked pained. "What if that's what we'll have together and we never find out because you leave?"

"Blake, listen to yourself. Do you realize what you're asking? Do you understand what I would be giving up? You're not hiring the band to stay on the tour, but you think that I should stay behind while they go on home? If you can look me in the eye and tell me that you think we have an irreplaceable love, that you could make a real commitment to me and to this relationship, then I will stay. I will give everything up. I really will, because I believe that finding your one true love is that important. It's too rare to pass up. But if you can't, then I'm afraid I have to go home. Listen, I know it's a lot to ask, and it's way too soon to be deciding if we love each other. I just can't give up my entire career for anything less. I hope you understand." Katie held her breath, hopeful that he would say the right thing, terrified that he would let her down.

This was soon, maybe too soon, to start talking about love, but he was asking her to give up everything else that she cared about. Surely he could understand that. She watched Blake open his mouth and then close it, hesitant to speak. His blue eyes were intense, full of emotion, and her heart swelled.

Katie was so sure that Blake would declare his love for her that she could almost hear the words. Blake took a deep breath. "I'm sorry sweetheart, but I can't tell you that yet. I care for you, a lot, and I want you to stay. I'm sorry."

Katie pulled her hand away from Blake's as though shocked. "You're sorry? Sorry? Just a couple of days ago you were telling me how you were hoping to find a wife. A *wife*. Now you can't even tell me that you think you might someday love me." She blinked, unable to move, unwilling to believe that she had just opened up her heart to him only to have him refuse her.

"I thought that you would want to stay with me, but I guess I was wrong. I can't promise you anything, and I guess I can't tell you what you need to hear." Blake's voice was so low that Katie strained to hear him. He seemed almost ashamed of himself. Katie let out a long, slow breath. She sat across from Blake, stunned, truly surprised that he had not offered more of an explanation.

"That's it? That's all you have to say to me? You know, Blake, *you know*, how difficult it's been for me to find someone who understands that what I'm doing with the band is a part of who I am, someone who won't be jealous or minimize its importance. You of all people should know where I'm coming from. The fact that you would so carelessly ask me to toss it aside for nothing in return is unspeakably selfish. I thought you were different. I really did, but it's clear to me that you're the same as every other guy."

There was no use in discussing it further. Katie had embarrassed herself enough, practically issuing an ultimatum, begging him to love her, and Blake had offered nothing in return. Nothing more than an opportunity to see if maybe they had something special, while she left her career behind and he continued to strengthen his. The more she thought about it, the more hurtful it became. He honestly thought that she would give up her chances of becoming successful with her band for a chance to ride around on his tour bus. *His* tour bus. *Her* bus would be rolling back to Texas and taking her career with it.

"I'd like to go back to my bus now. It's late, and I have a lot to think about," Katie said. She held her head high, determined not to cry or show how hurt she was despite her wavering voice. She had never laid her feelings bare like that before and to have them refused was devastating.

"Katie," Blake began, his eyes pleading. He reached out to put his hand on her shoulder and she shrugged out of his reach.

"No, I think I need to go. Please take me." She insisted, her voice calm despite the storm brewing inside her, threatening to break her heart. He looked like he wanted to say more but stopped himself.

"Okay," he whispered. Blake picked up his keys off the counter and made his way around the house, checking locks and turning off lights. "Let's go."

They drove back to the buses in silence, stubbornly avoiding eye contact with one another. Katie stared straight ahead as they made their way through Nashville traffic, concentrating on keeping her breathing even and her tears held back. She clasped her hands tightly together on her lap and promised herself that she would not cry in front of Blake. She had told him what she wanted from him, what she needed from him, and he had refused. He couldn't even offer an explanation, so there was nothing more to say. He obviously didn't feel as strongly for her as she thought, and she would not further humiliate herself by showing how much it hurt.

When they arrived in the parking lot, Katie was relieved to see a flurry of activity around the buses. The drivers and security team members were completing their safety checks and preparation for the drive to Memphis. That meant that they would be heading out soon and she would be one more show closer to the end of the tour by this time tomorrow night. She would put this tour and thoughts of Blake Jackson behind her.

Blake tried to take Katie's hand but she gently pulled away from him. "Can we talk about this?"

His voice was husky with emotion, but Katie resisted the urge to fall into his arms. She thought of all that she was leaving behind, how the rest of the world fell away when she was in his arms, her cheek resting on his chest, the stubble on his chin catching in her hair, and gave in to her tears. She drew the back of her fist across her cheek, swiping tears from her face, and forced herself to slide out of the truck. He seemed so vulnerable that Katie had to sternly remind herself that he had his chance but didn't take it.

"You know what? You say that you want someone who wants more than just the generic Blake Jackson experience, that you want someone who really knows you. Well that's me. *I* know you, and *I* want more. You refuse to offer it, though. All you're willing to give is the Blake Jackson experience and you refuse to open yourself up to something real. You can't have it both ways, you know. You'll never get anything more meaningful than what you've always had as long as you shut yourself off like this. So now, unless you have more to add than an apology, or you're asking the whole band to stay on the tour, then the answer is no. There's really nothing more to talk about." When he hesitated again, Katie spared Blake a sad, pained look and turned away before striding purposefully towards her bus.

Blake slammed his palms against the steering wheel and cursed in frustration before climbing out of the truck and slamming the door behind him. He watched Katie climb into her own tour bus before hanging his head and walking towards his own.

•••

Blake stepped into the cool, quiet air of his bus and looked around. He had so many nice things, so many small luxuries and comforts, and it was all so pointless to him now. He had worked so hard to make something of himself, to get all these things, and now he was alone. Alone in a fancy tour bus. He had devoted so much of himself to the business of being Blake Jackson that he had never bothered to find someone to share this life with.

Then along came Katie McCoy, offering nothing less than her love, and he ruined the whole thing. He was sickened by himself, disgusted by how casually he had treated Katie's career and how he hadn't had the nerve to just tell her how he felt. Three little words would have made her stay, but he would have had to open himself up, promise more than he was comfortable with, to say them. The opportunity was right there in front of him and he couldn't say the words. He simply couldn't let her bet everything on him. It was too soon to know if he loved her, and it wouldn't have been fair to tell her that he did.

It would have been so easy to let her believe that he was sure about her, sure about them, sure enough that she should leave everything important to her behind. He couldn't let her give everything up for someone like him. She was right to turn him down. She didn't know that he had never been in love, that he had never found anyone who made him feel the way she did. She didn't know that he had spent so much of his life building his career that he had never had a real relationship. If she did, she might have understood, might have given him more time to come around. She didn't know, though, and frankly she deserved better.

The bus driver stepped in and poked his head around the corner. "We're ready to roll out if you are, Mr. Jackson."

Blake sighed heavily. He had thought he'd be driving to Memphis with Katie, had pictured the two of them snuggled up together and excited about the adventure ahead of them. "Yep, let's go." He pushed his boots off and kicked them across the lounge before grabbing a beer out of the fridge and making his way to his bedroom. Alone.

Chapter Ten

Katie and her band played their best performance of the tour in Memphis, Tennessee. Although she had expected a sleepless night, she slept like a rock on the bus from Nashville and well into the morning after the band arrived in Memphis. Katie figured that she must have been drained by the extreme emotion of her night with Blake. The deep sleep protected her from her own misery, at least for one night, and refreshed her enough to put her chin up and refocus her energy on the band and the night's performance.

Katie wanted to lie in bed and cry, or raid the freezer for ice cream and call her mom to commiserate, but she had refused Blake's offer in favor of staying in her band. No use in losing her career, too. She usually rushed through a shower after the Sterling show so she could watch Blake's set afterwards, but not tonight. He had probably saved her usual special seat backstage, but it would be too painful to take it tonight.

Katie thought that surely the day would come when she would be able to see Blake on television or hear one of his songs without bursting into tears, but that day wasn't today. She lingered in her shower, turning the water as hot as she could stand it, standing in the stream as the tears she had been holding back all day finally came. If her band mates had wondered where Blake was all day, they hadn't said anything. None of them had even noticed that Katie was dying on the inside. She was either doing a great job of appearing normal or they just weren't paying attention. She hoped they wouldn't head out for the night without asking if she wanted to go. They might have already made their plans, but if Katie ever needed a night out with friends, and beer—lots of beer—tonight was the night.

She turned off the water and stepped out of the shower, pulling an oversized towel around herself. Scooping up her cell phone, Katie whispered a little prayer that the guys hadn't gone out for the night while she dialed Charles's number. She rubbed a towel over her wet hair while she listened to the phone ring.

"Well if it isn't Miss Katie McCoy," Charles drawled into the phone. "Thought you'd be watching Blake's set."

"Not tonight. I was wondering if you guys want to go out and get some beers. Blake's not coming. It'd just be us, like old times."

"Oh yeah, the good old days," he chuckled. "Before our little Katie went off and fell in love. Sure darlin', that sounds like fun. Come by when you're ready to roll."

"Thanks. I'll get ready fast and see you soon."

Katie ended the call and got to work on her hair and makeup. The results wouldn't be nearly as gorgeous as when she had her team working on her, but maybe it was time Katie remembered who she really was anyway.

• • •

Katie enthusiastically agreed to the dive bar the guys suggested, though it looked like a complete dump to her. When they arrived at The Snake Pit, she took in the rows of motorcycles parked in front and the parking lot full of dilapidated muscle cars and rusty pickup trucks with trepidation. The door opened as the band approached the bar, and loud heavy metal music and the shouts of a rowdy crowd spilled out from the bar into the parking lot.

Katie resisted the urge to take the nearest band mate's hand as they made their way inside. The guys probably had no idea what this place would be like when they chose it, but to Katie it felt like a challenge. It was as if they wanted her to prove to them that she was still one of them, not as separate from the group as the press would have everyone believe. Holding her head high, Katie pasted a bright smile on her face and walked in with her band.

The place was shabby and the crowd was rough-looking, but it wasn't nearly as frightening as Katie had imagined. The guys lining the bar and playing pool seemed like working class men blowing off steam after a long week, not menacing boogeymen out to get her. She relaxed and felt her smile become a little more natural as the guys found a table and Charles made his way to the bar to order shots for the group.

A night out with her band would help take Katie's mind off Blake and all that she had lost. It would help her remember what had been so important that she had let him go. The tequila shots that Charles brought for everyone were just what the doctor ordered.

Katie usually wasn't much of a drinker, but tonight was different. Tonight she desperately needed to feel like she belonged in her band. The guys had become closer, had spent so much time together the last couple of weeks that the divide between them and Katie was devastating. She wanted to find her way back. Back to her place in the group and back to herself. She gave the guys a wide grin and held up her shot glass in response to a toast Charles offered to the group. She swallowed her tequila, slammed her fist on the table and popped a wedge of lime between her teeth.

"WOOOO!" Katie shouted while her band laughed and motioned for another round. "That's what I'm talking about!" The guys laughed, and Katie loosened up. The divide between them was probably all in her head.

A waitress brought a tray of tequila shots and Charles asked for a round of beers for the table. Something caught his eye over her shoulder and he waved in the air, shouting, "Chet!"

Chet Wilson, Blake's fiddler, wove through the crowd towards the table, an open smile on his face. He shook hands with the guys in the band and introduced himself to Katie. "I believe we met your first night on the tour, but I'm Chet Wilson. I play fiddle for Blake Jackson."

"Of course I remember you, Chet! It's good to see you again." Katie shook Chet's hand and hid her confusion behind a bright smile. Since when did her band hang out with Chet Wilson? Chet pulled a chair over to their table and sat down right next to Katie. He offered her a friendly, easy smile, one that surely meant to reassure her that he was just here for the fun. Someone pushed a tequila shot towards Chet, and Jeff offered a toast.

"Here's to you, my friends," Jeff held up his shot glass. "May every day be happier than the last!" Jeff licked salt off his hand and drank his tequila in one swallow. Katie and the men raised their glasses in toast and took their shots after Jeff. Katie sucked in a breath after swallowing her shot.

"Maybe I should slow down," she admitted before sucking on a wedge of lime.

Charles laughed and nudged Katie's shoulder with his own. "Pace yourself, kiddo. We're just getting started."

The waitress approached their table and set down mugs of beer. Katie put her empty shot glasses on the waitress's tray and slid her mug closer. The tequila was already hitting her pretty hard, but she enjoyed the warm, loose feeling that was spreading through her muscles. She liked how little losing Blake bothered her right now.

She took a long pull of her frothy beer and sat back, looking around the table. The familiar faces should soothe her, should make her feel like she had made the right choice, but she couldn't help but notice how happy they all were, so completely oblivious to her heartbreak. True, she hadn't told anyone about her disastrous night with Blake, but did they really not notice that her world had crashed down around her? She took another drink of the beer and mentally shook away the negative thoughts. The alcohol was probably making her maudlin and she was determined to get over herself. Tonight was for fun, for getting back into the band's good graces and reaffirming that she belonged with them, not for wallowing in self-pity. She leaned in to hear Jeff finish a joke, one she had heard him tell dozens of times, and forced herself to laugh heartily with the group. With a few more big swallows, Katie finished her beer and set the mug down.

"Next round's on me," she announced to the table. The guys raised their mugs and cheered. Katie signaled for the waitress and said, "Beers and tequila shots all around, please. And see this handsome guy here? Bring him whatever he wants." She set a hand on Chet's shoulder as she spoke to the waitress, her words starting to slur.

Knowing that the guys had been spending time with Chet made her worried that they were looking to replace her, but she couldn't think that way. If it were any other guy from Blake's band, she wouldn't have given it a second thought.

"Hey, before I left, I heard that they found the guy who slashed the tires on your bus," Chet announced.

"Oh yeah? What's the story?" Charles asked as everyone leaned in to hear.

"As far as anyone can tell, it was just random vandalism. Some security guard caught a guy keying a car in a parking lot and when the police hauled him in, they ran his prints. They matched some found on the gate at the venue, so he actually ended up confessing. Everyone's still keeping their eyes open, but it looks like it's not something we have to worry about too much." Chet took a drink of his beer. "I imagine you'll be free to finish the tour without your bodyguard," he said to Katie.

"Aw, I'm going to miss him. My hair and makeup girls are crazy about Jonathan, and he makes great coffee." Katie giggled and took a sip of her own beer. Now that the danger had passed, she felt very foolish for assuming that she had anything to do with it. Like someone would go out of their way to target her, as if she was so special.

She leaned over and whispered in Charles's ear, "I need to go to the ladies' room. Save my seat, and make sure there's a drink waiting for me when I get back." She giggled as she swayed a bit in her chair.

Charles rose from his seat and held Katie's elbow steady as she stood. "Do you need me to help you?"

Katie shook her head seriously, though the alcohol had taken the edge off of her serious mood and made everything seem a bit silly. "No sir, I'm perfectly fine. See?" She walked to the ladies' room, standing perfectly straight, careful not to sway. She looked back and gave Charles what she thought was a jaunty little salute and was relieved to see him smiling at her indulgently.

Katie smiled brightly at other bar patrons as she walked past, as much to convince herself that she was having a great time without Blake as anything else. She doubted anyone recognized her, but she felt like everyone in the place was watching her.

• • •

Katie washed her hands and looked around the filthy bathroom. The mirror was cloudy and the walls were covered in graffiti, probably years' worth, where girls had come in and left their mark in permanent ink. She noticed a note scrawled close to an old scratched-up metal paper towel dispenser that proudly proclaimed, "I LOVE BLAKE". *You and me both, sister.* She hoped that the other girl had better luck with her Blake.

There were no paper towels, so Katie wiped her hands on her jeans and set her purse on the sink's edge. She pulled out a tube of lip gloss and concentrated on her lips in the mirror while she applied a fresh coat.

Satisfied, she made her way back into the bar and was halfway to the band's table when she heard angry, menacing shouting to her right. She turned her head just in time to see a pair of large men push up out of their chairs and tear into each other, fists pounding on one another as people around them scrambled to move out of the fray. A passing waitress was pushed into Katie, and they both hit the floor with a sickening thud as Katie took the brunt of the fall. The waitress had been carrying a full tray, but it went flying, sending mugs crashing to the ground, shards of glass pinging off the hard concrete of the floor as cold beer splashed all around them. Katie had slipped in the beer as the waitress hit her, making it impossible to keep her balance. Her head bounced off the smooth floor, giving her a brief flash of stars in her eyes, and the waitress landed on her, knocking the wind right out of her. She vaguely noticed the wetness surrounding her and wasn't sure if it was beer or if the glass had cut her.

Katie tried to lift her head but darkness bloomed in her vision, closing in from the outside and moving to the center as the ringing in her ears got louder and louder. Faces peered over her, faces that she could almost make out, and voices made noise that sounded like words, but Katie didn't resist when her body slipped into a buzzing, heavy sleep.

Chapter Eleven

Katie looked around the unfamiliar room, her eyes blinking against the harsh fluorescent light, her nose stinging with the antiseptic smell of the place before remembering where she was. She stretched in the small bed, wincing in pain and searching the bedside table for water. Her mouth was dry, her head was pounding, and her body was weak with fatigue. A nurse bustled in, smiling brightly as though Katie were a child.

"How are we doing this morning, hon?" The nurse strapped a cuff to Katie's arm and checked her blood pressure. She clipped a sensor to Katie's fingertip, and then she took her temperature with an ear thermometer. She looked over her clipboard down at Katie.

"I'm okay. My head hurts and I'm really thirsty. I guess I'm achy, too. Other than that I'm doing all right."

"You poor thing. I'll get you some water and see about some pain medication in just a minute. On a scale of one to ten, how would you rate your pain?"

Katie moved a bit in her bed, evaluating. "I'd say about a seven."

"I'm not surprised. You've been through an awful lot. The doctor will be in to see you shortly. Is there anything I can do for you besides get the water?"

"The light is really bothering me. If you could turn that off, I would really appreciate it."

"Sure thing, hon. You try to get some rest and the doctor will be in soon." The nurse refilled Katie's water pitcher and poured her a glass before turning off the overhead lights and leaving Katie alone, quietly closing the door behind her.

Katie squirmed and stretched in the hospital bed, careful not to pull out any of the monitor wires surrounding her. Her limbs were heavy with exhaustion, and her head was fuzzy beneath the pounding headache. She felt like she had run a marathon the night before, but it was not exercise that had her in this condition. She considered her arms and legs, evaluating, wondering how long it would take before she felt normal again.

She hadn't broken anything, hadn't even so much as sprained an ankle. She had fallen straight back, though, with nothing to slow her down, and when her head cracked against the unforgiving concrete floor at the bar, she had sustained painful bruising and what she thought was a mild concussion. She had been awake when they took her to the hospital, but it was difficult to remember the details amid all the chaos. The emergency room doctor who had evaluated her last night wanted her to stay overnight for observation, but if Katie remembered correctly she could expect to be fine with a little rest. Good thing, too, because rest was exactly what she wanted.

Katie was drifting off to sleep when a soft knock on her door roused her. A pretty young doctor entered the room, picked up Katie's chart, and said, "Good morning, I'm Dr. Patterson. How are you doing today?"

"I'm doing all right. I feel weak and achy, my head is pounding, and I'm still very tired. I think it could be a lot worse, though," Katie offered.

"That's true, Miss McCoy. You were pretty lucky. I've reviewed your test results, and you should be okay. You have a concussion, and there's the bruising and pain, but it doesn't look like anything is broken and we couldn't find any further injury. I'd say you are well enough to be released if you have someone who can keep an eye on you, just to make sure that you're safe. I understand that you're in a lot of pain this morning?"

Katie nodded. "My body feels like it's been hit by a truck, and I have the worst headache of my life."

"That's probably just bruising and strain from your fall, and I can order some pain meds for you. Today I'd like you to get plenty of rest, and I'd recommend that you follow up with your physician when you get home. I'll make sure that you get a list of symptoms and things to watch for. Do you have any questions?"

"I guess not. I'll let you know if I think of anything."

"All right then, Miss McCoy. I'll get your discharge orders started, and you can just relax in the meantime. While you're still here, use your call button if you need anything, even if you just want to get out of bed. That way, someone will be nearby to help if you feel faint or fall down. When you go home, be sure that someone is nearby to help just in case." With that, Dr. Patterson smiled and left Katie alone in her room again.

Katie took a sip of her water and laid back on her pillow, her eyelids heavy and her battered body begging for rest. The nurse bustled back into her room before Katie could slip into sleep again, a sympathetic smile on her face and a plastic cup holding tablets in her hand.

"Here you go, sweetie. Take these and we'll see if that helps." She offered the pain medication to Katie and helped her reach the cup of water. "You need anything else?"

Katie shook her head and fell back onto the pillow. "Thank you. I'm fine for now."

"All right, hon. You get some rest while you wait. It can take a while to get discharged. Do you have someone coming to pick you up?"

"Gosh I don't know. I'll have to make some calls."

"Okay. You do that, and I'll bring in your paperwork in as soon as it's ready." The nurse moved the call button closer to Katie and patted her hand. "Just press this button if you need anything in the meantime."

• • •

Katie didn't know how long she had been asleep, if it had been minutes, hours, or even days. She awoke to the sound of gentle snoring at her bedside and felt a hand covering hers, warm, gentle, familiar. Her eyes blinked against the soft light filtering in between the slats of the window blinds, and she stretched and moved in her bed, testing her body, checking for changes. Her movements woke Blake, who had fallen asleep sitting up at her bedside.

"Hey," he said softly, his voice heavy with sleep and emotion. "You're awake."

"You're here," Katie responded. "You came." She smiled weakly and squeezed his hand.

"Of course I came. Charles called me when they brought you in last night. I'm sorry, sweetheart, just so sorry about everything," Blake whispered. Tears welled in his eyes as he looked down at her.

"Me too," Katie answered in a raspy whisper.

"I can't help but think that this is my fault."

"I'm going to be fine. I've got a concussion, but nothing is even broken or anything. I'll get out of here soon, and all I need is some rest. I'm just disappointed about the tour. There's no way I can do the Georgia shows, and I hate to let the guys down."

Blake shifted in his chair and looked uncomfortable. Without meeting her eyes, he said, "You know Chet Wilson, the guy who has been playing fiddle for me? He's agreed to fill in for you so Sterling can stay on the tour."

"They've already replaced me? That was fast." Tears sprang to Katie's eyes.

"You haven't been replaced, he's just filling in for you so Sterling can stay on the tour. We cancelled tonight's show, but we're going to have to go on and get back on schedule tomorrow."

"The show must go on, right?" Katie was surprised by how bitter she felt. The biggest thing to ever happen to her career, and she had to miss it because of one stupid night at a bar.

"Please don't be like that. We can't cancel any more shows. It's too expensive." Blake looked pained and guilty.

"Yeah, can't let a little thing like a concussion get in the way of the tour. Good thing I didn't get really hurt. You might have had to cancel more than one show."

"Sweetheart, it's not just for me. When we cancel a show, we have to refund thousands of tickets. I have to think of the crew, the venue staff, the other musicians," he trailed off.

"I get it. It just hurts. I feel like I'm being left behind, and I worked as hard as anybody to get here. This is all I've ever wanted, and it hurts to get knocked out of the game just like that."

"I know, and I'm so sorry. I wish I could go back and change everything. I wish that this hadn't happened."

"But it did happen, and here we are. Nobody bothered to ask me if I could continue or if I needed a replacement. I'm not a child. I should at least get a say about what happens to me." Katie sighed and turned away from Blake.

"Nobody thinks you're a child. I know you hate that so much of this feels like business as usual, but our insurance won't allow us to keep you on the tour with the concussion. Just let someone else take care of you for a change, okay? You need help right now, and you have lots of people who care about you. Your parents are coming this afternoon and they'll take you home."

"What?" Katie screeched, sitting up in her bed, then wincing in pain. "My parents are coming? Why can't I just rest on the bus? It's not like I would try to get on stage before I'm recovered or anything. You say you don't think I'm a child, but that's hard to believe when you treat me like this, making yet another decision for me."

"Another decision? What's that supposed to mean?"

Katie frowned, afraid she was starting to pout but not sure how to stop now that she had said that. "I just feel like you've decided a lot of things for me. Our entire relationship has gone the way you want, depending on what you decide. You decided that if I didn't give up everything I ever cared about, it was over between us."

"What? If I remember correctly, you're the one who decided that it was all or nothing. I wanted you with me. I don't see how I could've made that more clear. I'm sorry you decided that wasn't good enough."

"That's not fair, and you know it. You can't ask me to choose between you and my career for nothing in return. You want me to just give up everything that I've worked for, but you can't even tell me that you might possibly someday love me."

"Katie," he stopped her. Despite her irritation she still loved the way her name sounded on his lips. "I'm no good at this and I just don't know what to tell you. When I asked you to stay with me, that's as far as I had thought it through. When it comes down to it, I just can't promise enough to justify you giving up everything. I can't let you throw away your life on me. I've never done this before, so I just think that I'm not a safe bet."

"Maybe you should let me decide that."

"I'm sorry. I can't be responsible for your entire future, you know? It's just—the stakes are so high and I was put on the spot, and I screwed the whole thing up. I care about you very much, sweetheart, and I don't want you to look back and wish that you hadn't taken a chance on me. If things didn't work out, I'd feel responsible for ruining your life. I wish we had more time to figure things out, but we don't. Now you're going home and I have to finish the tour and the whole thing just sucks."

"Who says I have to go home? Why didn't anyone ask me what I thought?"

Blake gave Katie an incredulous look. "Seriously? You think that you could do the shows? There's no way I'm taking that chance, sweetheart, and our insurance won't cover it. I called Luke and asked about concussions. He says that the best thing for you right now is rest. You won't know if you have any lingering effects until a couple of weeks have passed. You're lucky that you don't have any serious injuries, but we can't be too careful. You need to go home, get some rest, and make sure that you're all right. Your parents are coming today, in fact they're probably already on their way here from the airport. They were worried sick when I talked to them and they took the earliest flight out of Austin that they could get. They'll take you home and they'll take care of you until you've recovered."

"Okay, fine, maybe I can't get back on stage in the next couple of days, but who decided to call my parents? You? This is just more of the same. I'm not a little girl, you know. I'll be twenty-five years old soon, and I don't need you to make all my decisions for me."

"Sweetheart, I get that you're frustrated and that things obviously aren't going your way, but really? Yes, I was the one who decided to call your parents. Of course I did. Did you want me to just leave you here in the hospital to figure it all out for yourself? I was just trying to take care of you. If you hate it that much, then maybe I won't do it anymore." Blake pushed himself out of the chair and paced across the hospital room. He checked his watch and swore under his breath. "I hate leaving things with you this way, but I've got to go. I'm almost scared to ask, but would you like for me to get someone to stay with you until your parents get here?"

Katie looked up at Blake, sorry for her petulance, and sighed. "No. I'll be fine. Thank you for coming out here, thank you for taking care of me, and I'm sorry. I know that you're doing your best. I wish things had turned out differently."

He crossed the room back to Katie's bedside, took her hand in his, and leaned over to kiss her gently on her forehead. "Me too, sweetheart, and I'm sorry too. I don't want to leave you like this, and I don't think that we're done with this conversation. Take care of yourself, darlin'." With that, he left Katie alone in her hospital bed after sparing her one last, sad look, full of regret.

•••

Blake left the hospital wishing that he could have just a few more days to sort things out with Katie. Even a few more hours would have helped. She was so small and fragile lying in the bed, but she was certainly still feisty enough to argue with him. He laughed to himself, thinking only Katie McCoy would argue with him about whether or not she could perform with a concussion. What she lacked in practicality, she certainly made up for in spirit. Drive like that was what fueled his own rise to the top of his field, though a lot of good that had done him lately. How had he managed to ruin everything so quickly? It seemed like every decision he made with Katie was the wrong one.

Chapter Twelve

John and Sharon McCoy arrived at the Memphis hospital late in the morning and found Katie asleep in her bed. Tears sprang to Sharon's eyes as she watched her only child sleep. John drew in his breath sharply and tightened his hold on his wife's hand. Blake Jackson had called the McCoys the night Katie was hurt, had given them all the details, but nothing could have prepared them for the sight of her lying there. Her beautiful creamy skin was pallid with exhaustion and her arms were marred with angry, purple bruises.

Katie stirred, and her eyelids fluttered open. She blinked against the hospital room's fluorescent lights, confusion clouding her delicate features, and then relief dawned in her eyes when she recognized her parents. She didn't realize how homesick she was until she saw them standing there, side by side.

Katie stretched and squirmed in the narrow bed, smiled weakly, and said, "Y'all made it."

John McCoy took his daughter's hand and looked down at her, and his eyes full of worry. "We're here, honey. We're going to take care of you."

"How are you feeling, sweetheart?" Sharon McCoy looked at her daughter with concern. She ran her hands down the front of her neatly pressed shirtdress, an achingly familiar nervous habit.

"I'm all right. It's just a little concussion," Katie laughed weakly. "What would y'all do if something really serious happened to me? You look like you're about to faint." She kept her tone light, teasing.

"Well, we're going to take you home as soon as you get released, and you'll stay with us until you're better," said Katie's father. He took his glasses off and began wiping them with his shirttail, although there wasn't a smudge on them.

"I can't believe it, y'all. I should be in Georgia right now, getting ready for a show. This isn't how it was supposed to happen." Tears filled Katie's eyes and her mother handed her a tissue. "Everything's falling apart, you know? Nothing is turning out how I thought it would."

"I know, sugar. I know. Everything's gonna be all right," Sharon McCoy said softly as she smoothed Katie's hair behind an ear.

Katie's father shifted uncomfortably, and tried to lighten the mood. "So you met Blake Jackson, huh? He seemed really concerned about you when he called us last night."

"He's such a nice young man. He made all the arrangements for us so we could get down here as soon as possible, you know. All we had to do was pack our bags and show up. He had his assistant handle everything for us and he paid for everything," said Sharon.

"He really is a nice man. He's done a lot for me, and I never appreciated it. Now he's gone and I'm going home and I ruined the whole thing." Katie started crying again as her parents looked at her and each other quizzically.

"It's all right honey, nothing's ruined. Everything's going to be all right." Sharon patted Katie's hand and shushed her softly. "Just relax and try to get some rest. Daddy and I will go check on your discharge papers if you want. I'd like to get you out of here and into the hotel. It's got to be more comfortable than this hospital room."

"Okay. Do y'all already have somewhere to stay?"

"Mr. Jackson got us a hotel close to the hospital and a rental car. Like I said, honey, he took care of everything. All we had to do was show up." John gave his daughter a gentle smile.

"Of course he handled everything. He's a wonderful man." Tears threatened to fill Katie's eyes, but she was determined not to cry in front of her parents again. She was so ashamed of herself for berating Blake earlier. Everything he had done was because he cared for her. He had come through when she needed him most, had even helped her family, and she had rewarded him with petulance. Now he was gone, she was going home, and she had refused to even talk to him about their future. How could she have been so stupid? How could she demand all or nothing? Was there really no room for compromise?

To be fair, he was asking an awful lot of her when he wasn't willing to commit to anything more than staying together as long as it worked out. He couldn't very well expect the band to wait around to see if she'd return, to postpone their recording schedule, maybe miss out on important gigs. He couldn't ask her to leave her band, her career, and promise nothing more than a good time while it lasted. No, she was right to stand her ground. Maybe she was a little harsh in the delivery, but she was right to insist that her career be taken seriously. She knew that much.

● ● ●

Katie was released from the hospital that afternoon with instructions to take it easy, get plenty of rest, and to check with her own physician when she got home. Armed with a list of symptoms to watch for, she spent one restful night in Memphis with her parents before they all headed back to Texas.

After spending a couple of days doing little more than sleeping and waking occasionally to eat the meals that her mother prepared for her, Katie was feeling stronger and more clear-headed. She suspected that her exhaustion was due to her demanding tour schedule, constant travel, and the emotional devastation of losing Blake. Her injuries weren't even that serious, and she hadn't had any new symptoms develop from the concussion. The bruises from her fall were beginning to fade, her head no longer throbbed constantly, and she was able to stay awake for more than an hour at a time.

Things were looking up, and Katie was anxious to regain some semblance of her former life. It felt like it had been months instead of days since she and Blake and broken up, since she had boarded the plane to leave the tour and her dream behind. So much had changed, and Katie's heart pulled when she realized how much she missed Blake. Of all the things that had gone wrong in the past week, losing Blake hurt the worst. It was crazy to miss him so much when he had been in her life for such a short time, but Katie thought back to what Charles had said about time spent on tour being like a pressure cooker.

Alone in their little bubble, Blake and Katie had made a real connection, and Katie had found her perfect match. She missed his smile, his laugh, and the funny way he would hurry towards her when they saw each other. She pictured his exaggerated jogs toward her and smiled at the bittersweet memories. She missed being in his arms, and she still sometimes cuddled up with his shirt that she had kept so she could smell him. When she closed her eyes, that spicy, clean, distinctly masculine scent that was uniquely Blake brought back a flood of memories. She had given it all up, had given him up, to follow her career dreams. In the face of all that she had lost, how empty it had left her, her music career seemed insignificant.

She thought she had done the right thing, that she had worked too long and too hard to get where she was to give it up for nothing more than a few months on a tour bus. Surely she would get over him eventually, surely time would heal her broken heart, and she would be glad she had left. She would be grateful that she hadn't let herself get swept up in a romance that would end her career.

Right now, though, she was gutted. The pain of missing Blake was devastating, physical in its intensity.

•••

Blake was on his tour bus, halfway across Virginia heading towards Kentucky, when Luke called. He forced himself to shake off the melancholy feelings that hung over him and project a cheerful mood for his brother when he answered.

Luke dispensed with pleasantries and got right to the point. "Hey, can you do me a favor? I have a friend in Lexington who couldn't get tickets to your show. He has done a lot of work for the foundation, so I wanted to see if there's anything you can do."

"Yeah sure, that's no problem. I can have a pair waiting for him at the will-call window. I just need his name."

"Thanks, bro, it's Noel Campos. He's going to be so happy to hear that you got him those seats. I really appreciate it. So how are things? How's Katie? She feeling better?"

"Uh, yeah, I guess she's fine. I don't exactly know."

Luke was silent for a beat. "What do you mean, you don't exactly know?"

Blake cleared his throat. "Her parents took her home from the hospital, back home to Texas, and I'm not sure how she's doing now because I, uh, haven't talked to her since she left."

"What do you mean you haven't talked to her? Did you guys break up?"

"I don't know, exactly, I mean, yeah, I guess we did. I asked her to stay with me after Sterling left the tour, but she didn't want to quit her band. Then she ended up going home early anyway, and I guess that's it." Blake found himself wishing that he hadn't answered Luke's phone call. Hearing himself say it out loud made it even worse.

"What do you mean she didn't want to quit her band? Why would she have to quit her band? Did you give her some kind of ultimatum?"

"Well, no, it's nothing like that. I told her that I wanted her to stay with me, and she said that she couldn't because the band had gigs lined up and studio time scheduled after they were done with my tour. She didn't think that the guys would wait for her to come home, so she said no."

"So her only two choices were to stay with you and quit her band or go home and break up?"

"When you put it like that, it sounds pretty stupid. I wasn't sure what to do, and I obviously didn't handle things well. It just kind of fell apart."

"Wow. I'm sorry, bro. What did Mom and Dad say?"

"I haven't talked to them either. I'm afraid to tell them."

Luke snorted. "What are you afraid of? That they'll be mad?"

"Yeah, kind of. I know that they really liked Katie, and I screwed the whole thing up."

"How did you screw it up? I mean, besides being an inconsiderate idiot who doesn't call to check on a girl who went home with a brain injury?" Luke teased.

"You know, by letting her go home. She said that she would stay if I made a commitment to her or if I told her that I loved her."

"And you wouldn't? Because you don't love her?"

Blake let out an exasperated sigh. "Dude, I do love her. I was just caught off guard and thought it was too much responsibility and I froze. I didn't want to be responsible for her missing out on her career if things don't work out between us, and I guess I just panicked."

"Wow. Okay, so let me get this straight. A beautiful, talented, charming woman tells you that she will give up her dream job to be with you. All she wants in return is for you to love her, which you do, but for some reason you won't tell her. So instead of trying to fix things before it's too late, you let her go home without hearing a word from you? Am I missing anything?"

"No, that's about right," Blake mumbled.

"Okay, I just wanted to make sure I've got my facts straight before I tell you that you're the biggest idiot I've ever known. Have you considered that you had everything you've ever wanted right in front of you and you were too stubborn and selfish to make it work? How many times have you complained that you couldn't meet a woman who wanted to know the real you? I love you, man, but this is one of the stupidest things you've ever done."

"You're right. I've got to figure out some way to fix this."

"For your sake, I hope it's not too late. She really is something special, like once-in-a-lifetime special. If you don't take her, I will." Luke teased.

"Not a chance. All right. I've got some thinking to do. Don't tell Mom and Dad about this. I'll never hear the end of it."

Luke laughed. "I know that's right, they love Katie. I'm pretty sure Mom's already looking for a mother of the groom outfit for your wedding. I'll keep my mouth shut for you and save it for when I need to get you in trouble. Good luck, bro."

"Thanks. I'll have those tickets waiting for your friend. Talk with you soon."

Blake ended the call and put his head back against the seat. He looked out the bus window at the scenery flying by and silently berated himself for letting Katie get away without a fight. She was right about him, and she was right to leave. He knew how hard it had been for her to find a man who valued her career and didn't try to take her time away from it. He knew it and had the nerve to act like he was any different than the rest of the guys who weren't good enough for her. If she never forgave him, he would deserve it. He had to find a way to make it right.

• • •

Katie had been home over two weeks before she realized that nobody from Sterling had called her. She hadn't heard from Blake, either, but that was no surprise. She had pushed him away in the hospital and things had been so broken when he left that she'd be surprised if she ever heard from him again.

Not hearing from her band in all this time was a surprise, though. They should have returned from the tour over a week ago. She thought that they might feel distant from her since she had spent so much of the tour with Blake, but she still wanted to find out how everything had gone for the last couple of shows. Before the summer tour, she and the guys had practically been family, and surely that wasn't beyond repair. Ties like theirs weren't so easily broken. Why hadn't they checked in on her? They knew that she had been discharged from the hospital within twenty-four hours, but nobody even called to see if she was all right? Did they assume that since she went home everything was fine? What was going on?

She had been a good little patient since going home to her parents' house. She had gotten plenty of rest, she had visited her regular physician, and she had carefully watched for signs of trouble. There had been no new symptoms, her bruises had faded, and she was ready to get back to work. Everything was fine and she was getting restless. It was past time to return to her apartment, get back in the studio, put the mess with Blake Jackson behind her, and get on with her life. If the band didn't get back on stage soon she was going to have to find a job or beg her father for work at his office. Katie had bills to pay, and she was on her own again.

A few years ago, Katie might have quietly waited for them to call her, but this time she needed answers. She picked up her phone and called Charles. She thought it was going to go to his voicemail when he finally answered.

"Hey, Katie," said Charles.

"Hey stranger! You don't sound happy to hear from me." She tried to sound light and breezy, but she was afraid that her bitterness was showing.

"I'm sorry. Of course I'm happy to hear from you. How have you been?" Charles sounded contrite.

"I'm totally fine. I was released from the hospital, and I came home with my parents to recover. I've been resting and I haven't had any of the symptoms that the doctors told me to look out for. Now I'm feeling great and I'm ready to get back to work. How were the Georgia shows? Blake told me that Chet Wilson was going to fill in for me. How'd that work out?"

"They went really well, kiddo. We missed you, though."

"That's great. I missed y'all too. It was really disappointing to leave the tour with my parents instead of on the bus. So what's the plan? I haven't seen a current schedule or anything. I was going to wait for one of y'all to call me but I'm getting antsy."

Charles was quiet for so long that Katie thought the call might have been disconnected. "About that, ah, we have been trying to, ah, come up with the best way to tell you this, but, ah," he trailed off.

"What is it?" Katie asked. "Just say it, Charles." She wasn't sure that she wanted to hear what he had to say.

"We've run the numbers a dozen different ways, but it looks like we just barely broke even on the tour. Our expenses were much higher than we thought and it looks like it's going to be a while before we can afford to get back into the studio."

She let out the breath she had been holding. "Is that all? Oh my gosh, I thought something terrible had happened! You scared me!" She giggled.

"This is serious. We are way behind where we should be at this point. It's going to be a while before we can record any new material unless we come up with something soon."

"So what's the problem, exactly? Why can't we just juggle our schedule, play some gigs, and save some money before heading back into the studio? Not having tons of money isn't exactly new for us."

"Darlin', that's true, and chances are good that things will work out just fine. Jeff's having a real tough time with it though. He's real down about it, and I guess everyone is just disappointed. We all put so much into the tour and thought that it would make more of a difference. Now that we're home, it kinda feels like nothing has changed."

"I'm surprised to hear this. Y'all are usually much more optimistic."

Charles let out a big breath. "I know. We've just been at this for so long, and the tour was supposed to be the big reward for all our hard work. I'm sure things will start looking up once we get back at it. Maybe we're just tired."

"I'm sure that's a big part of it. I feel like all I've done since I got home is sleep. Let's get together soon and get back on track. Feeling sorry for ourselves won't solve anything."

"You're right, darlin'. I'll be in touch. See you soon."

They ended the call, and Katie sat back on the couch. She needed Sterling to succeed more than ever before. The guys in the band had no idea how much she had given up to stay with them, and she couldn't tolerate them moping around, whining about money and how much they didn't make on the tour. Her bills hadn't stopped coming just because she was out on a big summer tour, though, and she needed income.

Now what? Katie sat in her parents' cozy living room, surrounded by dated knick-knacks, familiar furniture and family photos, and wondered what she was going to do with herself. No gigs meant no money. No money meant that Katie had to figure something out quick.

Her father was always willing to hire her to help out at his office, so she could do that until things turned around for Sterling. Katie usually enjoyed working in his office, where she could help with the appointments, clean the sample eyeglasses, do a little filing. It wasn't enough of a plan for the future, though. She wasn't an optometrist's assistant, she was a fiddler. If Sterling didn't get enough work soon, she would have to get out and find bands looking for fiddlers to fill in, maybe get some studio work.

She tried not to dwell on the disappointment of coming home no better off than when they had left. When they found out they were joining Blake Jackson's summer tour, dollar signs and dreams of success had danced in her head. Now all she was left with were the memories. It was impossible to forget how Blake's arms felt around her, how his lips felt pressed against hers, how gorgeous he looked in the soft morning light.

Katie couldn't help but think about what she had given up to stay with Sterling. A couple of weeks ago, she had thought that her future in music was tied to these men. Now it looked like her future with Sterling was no different than her past with Sterling. With any luck, they had picked up some new fans, and maybe it would be easier to book more shows, better shows. Things probably weren't as bleak as Charles made them sound.

Chapter Thirteen

Blake had to figure out how to get Katie back. If his conversation with Luke didn't convince him, the excruciating emptiness in his heart did. The sickening weight of his loss stayed with him. It had landed in his stomach when he left her hospital room and it hadn't gone away. If anything it had grown worse. Every day that he spent away from Katie brought fresh pain, new reminders of what he was missing. He thought time would heal him, that having her out of sight would make losing her easier. He had to get her back, had to make it work somehow; if it didn't go well, he might be out of chances. He had to get it right the first time.

Chet Wilson's mother was critically ill, and Blake knew that Chet wanted to go to her but leaving the tour early would likely jeopardize his contract. Before Katie came into his life, Blake would have worked with Chet to find a temporary replacement while he tended to family matters. Chet would be allowed to return, confident that his job would be there waiting for him when his family situation was resolved. Blake was sorely tempted to let Chet go home and replace him with Katie. It could blow back on him though, perhaps in the press, almost definitely within the band. Everyone who played for him was hired for the job; they weren't a band in the traditional sense, but there was a family atmosphere that would certainly be disrupted if Blake let one of them go.

Blake had built a reputation in the music industry of treating the musicians who worked for him fairly, for creating an atmosphere of equality, of togetherness. So far nobody had challenged that or taken advantage of his inclusive nature. Replacing a long-time employee to suit his romantic desires could damage his reputation, but wasn't it his right? Hadn't he spent his entire career working to get to the place where he could pick and choose who played with him? Critical decisions require expert consultation. He picked up his phone and called Caroline.

"Hey, Caro, can you meet me in my dressing room?"

"Of course. I'm on my way. Give me two minutes."

Blake paced the length of his dressing room and ran his fingers through his hair. He gave himself a long, hard look in the mirror and pointed a finger at his reflection. "Don't mess this up," he said out loud to himself. He heard the clacking of Caroline's footsteps grow louder as she approached his room. She gave a perfunctory knock and poked her head inside the doorway.

"I'm here," she announced.

"Come on in and have a seat." He grabbed a couple bottles of water and joined Caroline at his table.

Caroline took off her blazer and draped it over the back of her chair before sitting down and opening the bottled water Blake offered her. She gave Blake an appraising look and he was sure that she was taking in the dark circles under his eyes and his newly gaunt appearance.

"Are you feeling all right?" she asked.

"I'm fine. I'm just tired. Have you heard about Chet Wilson's mother?" Blake asked.

"Yes, I believe he is interested in leaving the tour temporarily if you will give him leniency with his contract. Her condition appears to be worsening, and chances are pretty good that if you don't let him go, he'll leave anyway." She took a sip of her water and looked at Blake over the tops of her glasses. "I don't think you called me to discuss whether or not you should let him go though, am I right?"

Blake laughed. "Am I that transparent?"

"I just know you too well. I think I know where this is going," said Caroline. She gave him a sympathetic smile and put her BlackBerry on silent mode.

"So I guess I just need a voice of reason, I need you to talk this out with me. I will let Chet go, no problem. He can go tomorrow if he needs it. I can find someone to fill in, and as important as this tour is I still wouldn't keep a man from going to be with his dying mother. I want to let him go and replace him permanently, though, and I want a second opinion."

"You want Katie McCoy to replace him permanently but you're not sure if she'll do it, and you're worried about how that will make you look, right?"

"That's the gist of it. It feels like the right decision, and I know that I can do whatever I want, but I've worked hard to build this reputation. I don't know what to do, Caro, and I don't want to mess it up. I need a woman's point of view. Help me," Blake finished softly.

"Have you talked to Katie since she went home?"

"No. I hate myself for it, you know, but I haven't called. I didn't know what to say, so I chickened out. The last time I saw her, I messed things up so badly. God, I'm such a coward."

"Well, honestly, ignoring her for weeks doesn't look so good. I'm willing to bet that she was expecting to hear from you. I think that there's still hope, though."

"You do?"

"Sure I do. There's always hope. I saw how she looked at you. Katie McCoy is clearly a girl in love. Our problem now is that she's also a girl who has been let down."

"By me," Blake whispered. He ran his hands through his hair and let out a big breath, his cheeks puffing out.

"Well, sure, but don't be too hard on yourself. No use in going over the could-haves and the should-haves. It's time to think about how you can change things. From what you've told me, you asked

Katie to stay with you, but she wouldn't quit her band without a commitment, right?"

"That's right. I was so stupid, Caro. How could I have thought that she would give up everything else in her life for me when I offered nothing in return? All she wanted was for me to admit that I could see myself falling in love with her and she would have stayed. I couldn't even give her that. I'm such an idiot."

"When you say it out loud, it does kind of sound like she didn't have any other choice."

"I know. I was wrong and I get it. When the moment was there, I couldn't let her bet everything on me. I wasn't sure, I guess. I don't know. I've never had to do this before."

Caroline chuckled. "You've never had a woman challenge you before, huh? I guess most women are usually more than happy to do whatever you want. Katie's different, though. She demands more from you. Do you think you can rise to the challenge?"

"I really do. If I don't get her back in my life, I don't know what I'm gonna do. I'm miserable without her. I can't sleep, I can't think straight, I can hardly drag myself out of bed in the morning. It's terrible."

"Well, we could start by offering her the contract and letting Chet go," Caroline suggested gently.

"Do you think she'll take it?" Blake allowed himself to feel optimistic.

"There's only one way to find out. I can get the paperwork started, but I think that the offer should come from you. Of course we should hold off on handling Chet until you get an answer. That's going to be a whole different issue, and it might require some work on your part to repair any damage to your reputation. Be realistic, though, because this could be a tough road all around. Don't expect her to jump at the offer as soon as you call. I'm sure that she's been wondering why you haven't checked on her, and she might be pretty upset. You might have to grovel a bit, you know." Caroline smiled at the hopeful look on Blake's face.

"All right, I'll do it. I have to get her back. Don't say anything until I tell you. I don't want word to get out until it's settled."

"All right then. I'll leave you to it. Let me know what happens," she said as she stood to leave. She picked up her BlackBerry and her blazer and crossed the room. "Oh, and good luck," she said as she let herself out.

Blake held his phone in his hand, took a deep breath, and dialed Katie's number before he could chicken out.

• • •

Katie was polishing lenses in her father's office when her phone buzzed in her pocket. Her heart stopped for a moment when she saw the 615 area code. A Nashville number. *Blake.*

She had deleted his contact information from her phone after she had been home for over a week with no call from him. It was too painful to see his name when she scrolled through looking for someone else. She had told herself that she'd only get over him if she forgot about him completely. She hadn't listened to the radio or read any celebrity news since she had come home, but he was always on her mind anyway.

She stared at her ringing phone for a moment, not sure if she should answer or not. Knowing that she'd have a voicemail from him if she didn't was enough to make her take the call. She didn't want to be tempted to keep a recording of his voice, only to torture herself with it.

"Hello?" She tried to steady her voice, but was sure that she sounded as nervous as she felt. She looked down at the pair of glasses she was holding and saw that her hand was shaking.

"Katie, it's Blake." His rich voice came through the phone line and Katie felt like her knees would buckle from underneath her. "Don't hang up."

"I won't." Her voice trembled. She reminded herself to breathe. In and out. In and out.

"I don't know where to start, but I need to talk to you. Is now a good time?" He sounded hopeful.

"Sure, it's fine." Katie put the glasses she had been polishing back on the rack and went to her father's office for some privacy. She closed the door behind her and sat down at his desk. "I'm here," she said.

She heard Blake take a deep breath and let it out before he began. "First, I'm sorry. I'm sorry for how we left things, and I'm really sorry that I haven't called. I don't know why I didn't. Everything you said about me was right, and you were right to leave me. I've been thinking about you every moment since you left, and I guess I was just too chicken. I'm sorry."

"Thank you for that." Katie wanted to blurt out that she loved him, that she missed him, to tell him that she would take the first plane to wherever Blake was right now. It was time she let him do the talking for once, though.

"I feel like such an idiot. I never should have let you go like that, and I can't believe that it happened. I know that I haven't shown it, but I still care about you. I'm crazy about you, and I've been losing my mind since you've been gone."

"I still care about you too, and I've missed you. Being back home and not hearing from you once has been really hard." Her voice broke a bit on the last word. Saying it had been really hard was an understatement, but Katie couldn't bring herself to tell Blake that he had crushed her. "I'm glad that you called, though. It's really great to hear your voice again."

She heard Blake take another deep breath. "Wow, okay. So, here goes. I need a fiddler and I want to offer you the job."

"What about Chet?"

"His mother is really sick and he needs to be with his family. I need to fill his spot, and I'm sure we could find someone else, but

I don't want anyone else. I want you." Blake's voice was like a balm to Katie's frazzled nerves. It would be so easy to just say yes, to just follow her heart. She tried to remind herself how badly Blake had let her down, how hard it had been to put her life back together, but the pull she felt to him hadn't diminished a bit since she had come home.

"You need a temporary replacement?"

"That's where it gets tricky, and why you might not want to say yes. You know how my band is set up, the guys are hired to work and have no obligation to stay on after their contract ends. I've treated them like we're in a band together, though, rather than handle them like hired musicians. He'll probably expect to take a short leave and return when things are resolved with his family. In this case, I'd like you to take his place permanently, and I know that will bother some of the guys."

"You'd let him go for me?"

"I don't think you have to worry too much about Chet Wilson. He's been in the business a long time, and finding another gig shouldn't be a problem for him. It's not like I'd be throwing him out in the cold without a second thought. There will probably be some damage to my reputation, and there's a real chance that the band won't welcome you with open arms."

"I see. So you think I should leave Sterling to work for you in some hostile work environment?" She kept her tone light, teasing Blake as her mood improved.

"When you put it like that, it sounds pretty lame." Blake sounded adorably crestfallen.

"I'll do it." She surprised herself with the answer. Her rational side was telling her to hold out, to be practical, but her heart was the one that answered.

"Yes? You'll come?" Blake sounded so happy.

"Yes, I'll come. Where are you?" Katie smiled. Between now and when she arrived, she would have to get a hold on her heart, rein in her excitement, but for now she let the happiness wash over her.

"Kentucky. I'm in Lexington tonight, Louisville tomorrow. You can take as much time as you need, but the sooner you get here, the better. Just decide when you can join us and we'll let Chet go. He's under contract until I say differently, so it's up to you when you come on board. I'll ask Caroline to call you, and she can send you the contracts and make all your arrangements. She'll help you figure out what you'll need and can work out everything. I'll send Chet on his way just as soon as I know when you'll be here." Blake sounded like a kid on Christmas morning.

Katie laughed, and it felt good to be happy again. "Have Caroline call me, and I'll work it out with her. Thank you for the opportunity. I'll see you when I see you."

"Great, that's great. I can't wait."

"Me neither. See you soon." She ended the call and sat back in her father's rolling chair. A framed photo of her with her parents caught her eye. She was probably eighteen or nineteen and they were beaming at the camera on either side of her. They were so proud of her back then. Katie hoped that she would make them proud now.

Her real concern was leaving Sterling. She picked up her phone and dialed Charles's number, shaking with tension as she waited for him to answer. Her leg bounced so hard that she bumped her knee on her father's desk, and the framed photo of Katie and her parents fell over.

"Hey Katie," Charles answered.

"Hey." Katie had to tell them immediately; there was no time to waste if she was going to join Blake, but her throat closed around the words as she tried to tell Charles what she had decided. "I need to talk to you."

"What's wrong?" He sounded alarmed, and Katie took a deep breath.

"I'm leaving Sterling. I'm going to work for Blake. I'm so sorry."

Charles was quiet for a moment, as though digesting her news. "Well kiddo, this is a real surprise. I don't know what we're going to do without you. Are you sure about this?"

"I love him," she almost whispered. She cleared her throat and sat up straighter. "I'm sorry. I really am. I hope you find a new fiddler, someone even better than me." She laughed a little, a sad sound.

"You're irreplaceable, darlin', and I'm sorry to see you go. We can't compete with true love, though. Wouldn't even try." Charles's voice held a smile, its warmth reassuring Katie that their friendship wasn't lost.

"Thank you. I guess I'll need to suck it up and tell the guys tonight. I'm afraid they won't be as easy on me as you were."

"There's only one way to find out, you know. Best to do it quickly, like ripping off a bandage."

"You're right. I'll see y'all tonight. I'll try not to drive myself crazy worrying about it until then." They ended the call, and Katie slumped in her father's office chair.

Charles had always been easier to talk to than the other guys. There was every chance that they wouldn't let her off the hook as easily as he had. She was prepared for the worst.

•••

Four days after the call from Blake, Katie was on a plane to Indianapolis, Indiana to join the tour. Caroline had faxed contracts, schedules, sheet music, and lists full of information to Katie at her father's office. Katie's family physician had given her a clean bill of health, and her parents were excited for her.

She hadn't exactly given them the whole story when it came to her whirlwind romance with Blake Jackson. All they knew was that he was generous, caring, and concerned about their daughter.

Now he had offered her a long-term contract to work on a major tour, so he could do no wrong in their eyes. The McCoys had always been supportive of Katie's attempt to make a living in the music industry, but they seemed especially relieved now that she had a job with such a big act.

A flight attendant brought Katie the diet soda she had ordered, and she sipped from the plastic cup as she looked out the window over the clouds. As she left Texas behind, Katie tried to distract herself from thoughts of reuniting with Blake. She would have to keep things as professional as possible when she got to Indiana. She'd ride on the band's buses, she would attend rehearsals, she would do whatever she needed to do, but she would have to be much more careful with her feelings. Blake Jackson's band was the real deal, and there was no easy way out if things didn't go well between them. She would be on the road for six months with Blake and couldn't afford to have her heart broken again.

Maybe he was serious about wanting to mend things between them, maybe he would be ready to make everything right. All Katie knew was that she would wait to see what he did and said before she embarrassed herself again by wearing her heart on her sleeve. Sure, he was sorry that he hadn't contacted her when she went home, but she had to remind herself that he could have. He just didn't.

Katie didn't know if her heart could handle another dose of Blake's inability or unwillingness to commit. Forcing herself to move on with her life was hard enough when she was on her own, miles away from Blake. This time there would be no escape back home. This time she'd be forced to see him every night on tour, mere feet away from her on the same stage.

Katie looked down on her tray table at the beverage napkin she must have shredded. She took a deep breath and wished that she had asked for rum in the diet soda, or that she knew how to meditate or something. Why did she think that she could throw herself back into the relationship pressure cooker with Blake? Who was she kidding? And why didn't she stop to think about what it would be like to be on the road with a brand new band? Would they even like her? Would they miss Chet and resent her? Could she even do this? Sure, Katie knew Blake Jackson's songs, but she had never played them with anyone, only alone in her house. She slumped in her chair and groaned. So much for being rational.

The flight attendants walked up and down the aisles collecting cups and napkins, and the pilot turned on the fasten seatbelt sign. Katie put her tray table up and returned her seat to the upright position. Now she was minutes away from seeing Blake again, from being reunited with the one who made her heart sing. Her knuckles were white from gripping the armrests and her heart was racing. She forced herself to let go of the armrests, slow her breathing and relax.

Katie gripped her carry-on bag and forced one foot in front of the other as she made her way along the jet way with the other passengers and through the airport to baggage claim. She composed her features into what she thought was a neutral expression, squared her shoulders, and looked around for Blake.

Hundreds of travelers bustled around Indianapolis International Airport, families reuniting, soldiers returning from duty, businessmen carrying briefcases, but Blake Jackson was nowhere to be seen.

Katie stood with her luggage in the crowded baggage claim area and scanned the faces in the crowd, searching for Blake. Eventually she noticed a distinguished-looking man in a tailored suit holding a small placard that read "Katie McCoy". They had sent a driver for her. Of course. Why had she assumed that Blake would meet her? *Sure, Katie, the country's biggest star is just going to take a little break from his busy day and come pick you up at the airport. Idiot!*

She made her way towards the chauffeur and introduced herself. He helped her with her bags and they made their way out into the parking lot. Katie looked at her driver and exclaimed, "Oh my gosh, what a gorgeous day!" He looked at her with amusement. "Well, it was a hundred degrees at home yesterday, so this is practically sweater weather. Y'all don't know how good you have it here," she explained.

"Oh yes, you came in from Texas. Well then, I hope you'll enjoy Indianapolis. Here's your car, Miss McCoy." He led her to a spotless black Lincoln Town Car and loaded her bags into the trunk after she slid into the backseat. Katie settled in for the ride as her driver merged into the traffic on I-70, and lay her head back on the seat and watched the scenery in silence as they sped towards Lucas Oil Stadium, relieved that her reunion with Blake had been postponed for the time being.

Chapter Fourteen

About half an hour later, Katie arrived at Lucas Oil Stadium and gawked at the huge venue in disbelief. Never in her wildest dreams had she ever played anywhere even half this size! Of all the stops for her to join the tour, this was by far the most intimidating. She spotted Blake's tour bus in the lot and wondered if he was on board. Her legs went a little wobbly in her boots at the thought of being so close to him.

She forced herself to gather her bags and look ahead when the memories of her time with Blake inside that bus crept into her mind, causing her body to tingle all over. Katie sternly reminded herself that it was time to rehearse like the professional she was if she was going to make it on this tour. She let assistants handle her luggage while she strode across the lot to meet Caroline Mathers.

"Katie, hello. Welcome! We are so pleased that you could join us. How was your flight?" Caroline gave Katie a firm handshake.

"Great, thank you. I'm glad to be here."

"Wonderful, well, I am sorry that you don't have more time to get settled before you get started, but the schedule is very tight. I'm afraid you'll just be thrown right in to the thick of it this afternoon. I'll get someone to take your things to the bus and you can get settled in later. You'll have enough time to get what you need before the show. The band has already set up for a rehearsal inside, and they are ready for you." Caroline led Katie into the venue and on to the stage, where Blake's band was set up and waiting.

Katie gripped the handle of her fiddle case and swallowed her fear with an audible gulp as she made her way up the steps to the stage. *You can do this. You've played these songs for years and you are a professional.* She pasted a friendly smile on her face, hoping to hide her nervousness, and joined the band on the stage. "Hi everyone, I'm Katie McCoy."

Blake's band greeted her with friendly reserve and she wondered if they had been told that Chet was not coming back or if they thought she was a temporary replacement. Were they unhappy to have her on tour? Did they resent that Blake was playing favorites? As if it wasn't stressful enough to join such a huge act right in the middle of the tour, now there might be tension between her and the band?

A door opened and Blake strode in, heading straight for the stage. Seeing him again brought a rush of emotion so powerful that Katie swayed on her feet for a second. He bounded up the steps and cleared his throat. "I see y'all have met Katie McCoy, our new fiddler." He gave Katie a brief glance that set her heart racing before addressing the band. "Before any rumors get started, let me just tell you guys that Chet has gone back home to be with his family indefinitely. His mother is very ill, and he didn't want to be on the road when he should be with her. He wanted to take a leave, he wasn't fired, but I have chosen to terminate his contract altogether. He will not be returning, and you can consider Miss McCoy our permanent fiddler." Blake gave the band a level stare as they grumbled, then continued on as though he hadn't heard them. "Y'all might remember her from other shows. She used to be with one of the openers, Sterling. They were with us in Alabama, Tennessee, and Georgia. We're all going to miss Chet, he was a great fiddler, but Katie is an excellent musician and will be a great addition to the group. I expect that you'll help her get up to speed. Everybody got that?" He challenged them to object with a direct look to each man in the group.

The men nodded and mumbled their welcomes to Katie. She smiled as enthusiastically as she could and said, "Thanks y'all. I'm really happy to be here and I'm looking forward to working hard." She tried to catch Blake's eye, but he was deliberately ignoring her.

"All right, let's get started." Blake took his place at center stage and the band ran through the set list. Katie organized her sheet music and equipment around her and got to work with the rest of the band.

The rehearsal was exhausting. Between the flight, Katie's nerves over seeing Blake again, and working so hard to play as well as the rest of the band, she was ready for a nap by the time Blake dismissed everyone to get ready for the show later that night. Katie was thankful that she already knew most of the songs, but playing along with the radio and playing in the band were two different things. She'd also never played in a stadium before. This was probably the biggest show on the tour, and Katie berated herself for not delaying her arrival one or two more days so she could start somewhere smaller. She was packing up her gear when Blake approached her.

"I'm so glad that you're here, and it feels so good to see you again. I don't have much time to talk right now, but I really want to meet with you later. Please be patient with me for a while. The guys are kind of upset about me letting Chet go, so I think it's probably best that we lay low when we're in front of everyone for now." He looked around and, seeing nobody, dropped a tentative kiss on her cheek. "I missed you so much."

The kiss went straight through Katie, sending a zing of attraction right to her toes. "Me too."

He checked his watch and groaned. "Our schedule is tight today, so I gotta get moving. You sounded great in rehearsals, but just in case, I ordered a screen prompter for you. It's like a teleprompter but it displays music. You'll be able to see the screen but to the audience it looks like the rest of the stage gear. That way you don't have to worry about messing up while you're still learning the songs."

"That will be really helpful, thank you. I have never played anywhere near this size, so to be honest I was kind of wishing that I hadn't come for this show. My nerves have been fried. This will make things a lot easier."

"I'm glad, sweetheart. I also just want to assure you that I'll never let our personal situation affect your job with this band or on this tour. I know how important your career is to you, and I want you to know that whatever happens between us won't affect your job here." He shifted nervously and looked at her hopefully.

"Thank you. That means a lot to me, and I'm really looking forward to working with you." The tension, the strange situation, the unknown future—it was so stressful. Katie wanted to grab onto Blake and never let him go, but it was almost a relief when he left and she was free to prepare for the show on her own.

• • •

Blake slumped on the couch in his dressing room and stared at the ceiling, motionless. He didn't know how he would react to seeing Katie again, but he never imagined that he'd be so stiff and ridiculous. He could just hear himself telling her that their relationship wouldn't interfere with her job, and he felt like an idiot. He should forget about the other guys, pull her into his arms, and beg her for forgiveness.

She was so beautiful on stage during rehearsal, so clearly in her element. He would have to pull himself together if he was going to work alongside her for six months. Would she take him back? Would it be better to wait until the tour ended? Seeing her this afternoon assured Blake that his feelings for her had not changed except to grow stronger. He felt the same magnetic pull towards Katie, the same undeniable attraction to her. One look at her affirmed that he had made the right decision in asking her to join him on tour. Fortunately for him, she was as talented as she was beautiful. Unfortunately for him, the hurt lingering in her eyes was caused by him and his stupid inability to commit.

He didn't know how he was going to do it, but he did know that he couldn't mess things up with Katie this time. He thought calling her to hire her was hard. Now he had his work cut out for him.

•••

A knock on her door woke Katie from a nap on the little couch in her dressing room, and she stretched, feeling like she had been asleep for days instead of an hour. Her body ached and her mouth felt like she had been chewing on a sweater, but it was time to get ready for the show. Tiffany and Cara stepped into the doorway, matching expectant smiles on their faces.

"You guys! What are you doing here?" Katie hopped up, forgetting how sore her muscles were and how foggy her head had felt. "I can't believe it! You're really here! How can it be?" She squealed as she rushed over to the hairstylist and makeup artist and pulled them into a big hug.

Tiffany laughed, "Girl, when Blake Jackson called, I came running."

"You know it. Well, actually his assistant called, but I think it was his idea. He thought you might like a couple of familiar faces when you got here," Cara added.

Katie's eyes shone with tears. "I'm so glad that y'all came. I'm excited to be here, but I have to admit, it has been so hard. I don't really know anybody and I can't tell if they want me here or not. Blake kind of let the other fiddler go to bring me here, and it's not going over with the rest of the band very well."

Cara sucked in a breath. "Ooh, awkward."

Katie laughed without humor. "Tell me about it. So there's that, and it's weird to be back with Blake. We hadn't spoken once since I left."

"Wow, really? Last time we saw you two together, you guys were like two peas in a pod. Did you break up or something?" Tiffany asked.

"Yeah, I guess we did. We couldn't really agree about what we would do when my band was finished with the tour and things just kind of went downhill from there. I'm sure you know that I had a bad fall and ended up in the hospital, right? Well, that's why I had to go home early. I ended up with a concussion and had to take it easy for a couple of weeks. Blake's fiddler replaced me for the last couple of Sterling's shows so they finished up without me. One thing led to another and now here I am, working for Blake."

"So now what? Think you two will get back together?" Cara finished setting up her products on the vanity and started working on Katie's hair.

"I don't know," Katie said. She looked down at her hands in her lap and sighed. "To be honest, when he called to hire me, I really thought we would. I tried not to let myself get carried away, but of course I thought we would. I think I really want to, but I'm not sure."

Tiffany's brow furrowed as she applied Katie's makeup. "You think you might not get back together?"

"I really don't know. I have to be really careful this time, really consider everything before I decide what to do. It's hard, because I love him, he's my heart. It's like when he's gone I can't breathe. I left my band to be here though, and I had been with them for six years. That was a lot to give up, and there's no going back for me now. I have to be really careful with Blake, because now he's my boss. If things don't go well this time, he could fire me, or at least make things really uncomfortable for me. I didn't really think it through before I made my decision. I was just hoping that he felt the same way that I do and that maybe he would have missed me so much that he would have changed."

"Hmm, well I don't know what's going to happen, but one thing I can tell you for sure, you made the right choice. The last time I saw you two together, Blake Jackson looked like a man in love, and I've only seen a man look at a woman the way he looks at you in movies. You can't fake that in real life," said Tiffany.

"Well I guess we'll see. I have to figure out how to work with him no matter what happens."

Tiffany and Cara finished Katie's hair and makeup and said their goodbyes. They stepped aside, giggling, as Blake came in as they were leaving.

"Perfect timing. We just finished hair and makeup." Katie turned to Blake and smiled shyly.

"I see that." He eyed her appreciatively. "You look gorgeous."

"Aw, thank you. Well, come on in. What's up?" Katie was being artificially casual, but she wasn't going to throw herself at Blake.

"I just wanted to see you before the show. I still can't believe you're here." They sat on her little couch together and he took a strand of her hair between his thumb and finger, rubbing it absentmindedly as he looked into her eyes. "I never got a chance to see how it went with the Sterling guys."

"Oh, them." Katie frowned and took a deep breath. "It was pretty harsh. I told Charles about it first, and he was so understanding and sweet about it that I mistakenly thought the other guys would be okay with it. It was truly awful. I was hoping that we could all be friends, that maybe we could work together again in the future, something. I don't think they'll ever want to see me again."

"That bad, huh?"

"Yeah. They were really mad. The band is struggling, financially, and we—or they, I guess—need to wait before going back into the studio. Everyone was already kind of down about everything, so this was just like more bad news. They were pretty resentful that I was moving on to a bigger act while Sterling still has to struggle."

"I'm so sorry. I wasn't sure which way it would go with them. It it's any consolation, my band was pretty ticked off, too." He smiled ruefully.

"Well, you can just fire anyone who gives you a hard time." She punched him playfully on the shoulder.

"I should do that, maybe just remind them who's boss," he said with a smile. "Seriously though, it's probably my fault. I always thought I was doing the best thing by treating my musicians like we were in this together, but when it comes time to make tough decisions it goes down harder. It's not easy for them to go from seeing me as the singer in their band to their boss."

"Well, I'll be extra careful, then. Don't want to blur any lines."

Blake took Katie's face in his hands and gently placed a soft kiss on her lips. "You are the exception." Reluctantly, he got to his feet and walked to the door. "I'll see you tonight."

Chapter Fifteen

Katie felt like she had been baptized by fire the past week after joining Blake's tour, but things were smoothing out and she was hitting her stride. The music was coming more naturally to her, the guys in the band seemed to be starting to respect her as a musician in her own right, and every day she felt more confident.

It was so tempting to reach out and touch Blake every time they were together, but he treated her with professionalism and painstaking equality when they were with the band. It was almost physically painful for her to keep her distance from him, but now that the band was starting to bring her into the fold, she was so glad that she had. If they believed she was there as Blake's girlfriend, her life on the road with them would be miserable. Her heart still skipped a beat when she saw him, and she longed for the day when they could have a chance at a normal relationship.

Katie was resting in her dressing room in Wichita, Kansas, after Tiffany and Cara had finished transforming her for the show when Caroline Mathers stopped by. "Katie, Blake would like for you to see him in his dressing room as soon as you can." Caroline's carefully arranged neutral expression revealed nothing.

"Hmm, okay. I'll be right there. Thanks." Katie wondered if there was a problem.

She gave herself a quick look in the mirror and applied a fresh coat of lip gloss before heading down the hallway to Blake's dressing room. She knocked on the door, which was already slightly ajar.

The door opened to reveal Blake standing in the middle of the room surrounded by soft candlelight. Katie walked in and turned around in a slow circle, taking in the candles filling Blake's room. He had placed about a dozen candles in small jars on every flat surface of the room. Blake offered Katie a flute of pink champagne and led her to the couch. They sat side by side, and he looked at her with hope in his eyes.

"First, I want to tell you how glad I am that you're here, and how sorry I am for everything that's happened. I have been so scared that I would mess things up with you that once you were here I didn't know what to say. I know that you were probably expecting something different, and once again I didn't deliver. I feel like a fool for how I've behaved, and I want you back."

Katie took in the scene that Blake had constructed, breathed in the heady amber scent of the candles, and took a sip of her champagne, feeling bubbles tickle her nose. Everything was beautiful, a perfect scenario. She thought that any girl in America would be happy to be in her cowboy boots right now. It would be so easy to say yes and go back to the way things were. It felt right, and Katie wanted to be with Blake. Just being in the same room with him made her nerves tingle with excitement. Everything about Blake was made just for her, like he was the perfect fit. She had worked so hard to find the place within herself where she could work alongside Blake without tasting the bitterness of his refusal to commit, but all she wanted to do was surrender to his touch now that he had said he wanted her back. She wanted him back too, but she hadn't forgotten the dark days of loneliness she suffered through during the weeks at home in Texas with no communication from him. It would take more than candles and champagne to assure her that he wouldn't hurt her all over again. As much as she ached for Blake to be back in her life, it had been too hard to let him go. She'd have to be sure that he was sincere.

"I don't know. I don't think I'm quite ready. This is lovely," she gestured around the room. "It really is. I know that I'm lucky to be here, but you know, you've really hurt me. When you let me go, my world stopped. I felt like my heart had cracked wide open. Everything was darker without you. When I was at home and didn't hear from you even once, I thought I would stop breathing. But I didn't. I picked myself up, all on my own, and now I'm starting to feel normal again."

"I'm so sorry. I'll never forgive myself for how I treated you. You deserve so much better, and I want the chance to give it to you." Blake's eyes were pleading.

"I appreciate that, and I forgive you. I really do, and you don't have to be sorry any more. But I can't forget it, at least not yet. I have to be realistic and ask myself if this would be happening if you hadn't been able to hire me. If you didn't need me in your band, would we have ever spoken again?"

"Of course we would," Blake insisted. "I risked losing the respect of the rest of the band to bring you here. I let a great fiddler go for you. I risked my reputation for you, and I didn't do that on a whim."

"I appreciate all that, I really do, and I don't take it lightly. I'm just not entirely convinced that it would have happened if Chet didn't need to take the time off. Remember that before you brought me back, you had to let me go. You let me go home because I couldn't give up my entire life to be with you. You couldn't see past your own wants and needs to try to meet me halfway. I hate to say this, but it really felt like you thought of yourself first. When things got tough, you didn't really consider my needs. It seemed like if it couldn't be on your terms, you didn't want a relationship with me."

Blake took her hand and stroked circles against her skin with his thumb. "I'm so sorry, sweetheart. I didn't think that I was a good enough bet, and I didn't want you to take the chance on me. I've never done this before and I know that I screwed it up. I can see that I have been so selfish, and I'm ready to change."

She squeezed his hand. "I hope so. I've changed, too. I'm not going to give my heart to someone who won't keep it safe. I want and need a real commitment, and I don't want to beg for it. I love what we had together, but I don't want it back if it's not for real."

"We can have that again. We could go back to the way we were. We're here together now, and we can stay together."

"I'd like to think that, but I need more time before I'm sure. We're only together here because you had a convenient way to make that happen. I certainly appreciate it, don't get me wrong, I am so grateful for the opportunity, but I have to be careful with my heart. As far as I know, you could have gone the rest of your life without ever calling me again. I'll need time to see if this is more than a convenient situation for you. If you don't want to wait, then I'm sure there are a hundred other girls who would be willing to take whatever you'd be willing to give them."

Blake smiled, as though he sensed that he had a chance. "I don't want any other girls. I want you, only you, and I'll prove it to you."

Katie kissed Blake softly on the lips and whispered, "I hope so."

•••

Blake made his way around the dressing room, blowing out candles, dazed in disbelief. He had known that it might be awkward between him and Katie, but he thought the champagne and candles would put her in a more romantic mood.

He wished that he hadn't been so awkward and stiff around her when she first joined the tour. Surely she was expecting a warmer reception, and then what she got was Mr. Businessman. She obviously needed to see that he could change, that he could put someone else's needs above his own. He had to find a way to make her believe that he could commit.

Blake wished that he had a sister or even a close female friend who could help him with this. He needed a big idea, like a grand gesture, to win her back. He thought the candles and champagne would do the trick, but he apparently underestimated how badly she had been hurt.

• • •

Katie quickly rounded the corner and made sure she was out of Blake's eyesight before she let herself slow her steps to a more normal pace. She relaxed her shoulders and took a few deep breaths as she approached her dressing room. Once she was safely ensconced in the privacy of her room, she locked the door and sat down on her couch. She wanted to fling herself face down on the cushions but Tiffany and Cara had worked so hard to perfect her look that she hated to ruin it.

So, Blake wanted her back. Now what? Katie imagined how delicious it would feel to be back in Blake's arms, feeling his breath tickle her earlobe as he whispered sweet words to her. It would feel perfect to be back by his side, and part of her wanted to forget about waiting and just jump back in to the relationship. Everything was right when they were together. It was as if Blake was made for her, like she had found her perfect match.

She thought of the dark days following her return home to Texas, how many hours she sat alone, wishing he would call. It seemed to have been so easy for him to forget about her. Of course, she didn't know if he had forgotten about her or if she truly just didn't know what to do. She decided that there was no reason that she couldn't eventually move past what had happened, but she would need evidence of a big change in Blake. She needed to see that he wouldn't take her for granted again. He would have to show her that he had grown enough to think of someone other than himself, that her heart would be safe with him. She just hoped that she keep herself from throwing herself in his arms long enough to make him work to get her back.

She looked at herself in the big dressing room mirror, at her expertly applied makeup and shiny, bouncy hair, and realized that she hadn't given Blake enough credit. He had made the arrangements for Tiffany and Cara to join her on tour, at his own expense, as a way to make Katie more comfortable. He figured that she would need a couple of friendly faces when she arrived, and had made this happen for her. It was entirely possible that Caroline Mathers had given him the idea, but Katie chose to believe that Blake thought of it all himself. She picked up her cell phone and dialed Blake's number.

"Katie!" Blake answered, sounding achingly optimistic.

"Hey. Listen, I just wanted to thank you so much for bringing Tiffany and Cara on board for me. I never thanked you for that, and I want you to know how much it means to me. I was so excited to see them, and everything has been so overwhelming for me that it is wonderful to have them here with me."

"It's my pleasure, sweetheart. I'm glad that you're happy. You know, if you decide to give me the chance, I'll do many more things to make you happy." Katie could hear the smile in Blake's voice. He sounded lighthearted, but she hoped that he was completely sincere.

"Keep it up, Mr. Jackson, and I might have to find out." Katie kept her tone light, but she wondered how she would ever hold out long enough to be sure that he had changed.

"I plan on it. You wait and see."

Katie laughed. "Okay, I'll hold you to that. See you at the show."

"See you tonight, sweetheart." Blake ended the call.

Katie held her phone in her lap and felt a huge grin spread across her face. Even after all they had been through, she still loved Blake. It would be torture to keep him at arms' length for much longer, but she just couldn't give herself to him as freely as she had in the past without making him wait, at least a little while.

• • •

Blake hummed to himself as he completed his last-minute preparations for the show. Katie hadn't taken him back, but he thought he could hear traces of affection in her voice. He was confident that he could win her back with a little effort. He decided to stop feeling sorry for himself, to stop wishing he could change the past, and start looking towards the future.

Hiring Tiffany and Cara to join Katie for the rest of the tour was expensive, but clearly worth every penny. Blake was glad that he had thought of it, and even more glad that it helped Katie. It was a step in the right direction, but Blake had a feeling that he should do more than just give Katie nice things. A girl like her cared more about what a person did, how he used his resources to help others, than how many gifts he could buy her or how many fancy dates he could pay for. He already sent money to Luke's foundation regularly, but that was easy. Katie wouldn't be impressed by him writing a check to help his brother's foundation. She would be impressed if he took the time to find other ways to use his money and celebrity to help others, and he had the beginnings of a great idea.

He called Caroline on her cell phone. "Hey, Caro, can you do me a favor?"

"Of course," she answered.

"If you have time, would you poke around and find information on local shelters for battered women and children? I need it pretty quick."

"Sure, I can do that. How quick are we talking?"

"Actually, like right away if you can. I know that we'll have to move on this immediately, but if we can get something out by the time the doors open tonight I would appreciate it. Here's the thing. I want to get the contact info for the organization, get donation boxes out around the venue, and get the folks coming in tonight to donate to the cause. I'll match whatever they put in, or double it, or whatever. I haven't thought it all the way through, but I want to start tonight, and I want to think ahead and do it in other cities too." He stood up and paced around his dressing room, energized by the idea and excited at the potential.

"I'm searching online right now. Is this the new and improved Blake Jackson?" Caroline asked affectionately.

"Yep. I hope you're ready, because I'm making some changes."

She laughed. "Does this have anything to do with Katie?"

"Well, I'm hurt that you would think that," Blake joked. "But yeah, Katie seems to have gotten the idea that I don't think of anyone but myself. I'd hate for her to be right."

"You're a good man. I'm sure she'll see that. Okay, so I have some results from my search. I'll call around and get everything set up. I'll have the details for you before the doors open tonight."

"Sounds good. Thanks for your help."

•••

The band had just finished their first song of the night, Blake's popular hit 'Someone like You', and Blake stood at the microphone. "Hello, Wichita! Thank you for coming out tonight!" The audience cheered so loudly that Katie could feel the vibrations under her feet. Blake waited for the crowd to quiet down, and then said, "We've got a lot of music coming your way tonight, but first I wanted to take a moment to thank you for helping me. I know y'all saw the pink boxes out in the lobby, and I know that many of y'all donated money when you came in. I thank you, and the YWCA Women's Crisis Center thanks you. We will be total-ing up your donations at the end of the night, and I will match them!" A cheer went up from the audience. "Thank you! I thought it was high time I gave back to the communities that have given me so much. Thank you for digging into your pockets tonight!"

Blake grinned at Katie and winked. She tucked her fiddle under her chin and flashed a toothy smile at him.

"How do ya like me now?" He mouthed the words to her, nodded to the band, and counted "One, two, three, four!" before the band launched into their next song.

...

"You really are something, you know that?" Katie fished a bottle of water from a tub of ice in the band's hospitality room and wiped it on her jeans.

"You liked that, huh? Well, there's more where that came from." Blake took a drink from his own water bottle and gave Katie a wink.

"More? How many times can you match an entire audience's donations before you go broke?" She grinned up at him.

"Well now I didn't say that I would do the same thing in every city," he laughed. "I'm just trying to use my powers for good, you know? Helping others, being a good guy, all that stuff."

"I'm just giving you a hard time. I think that what you did was amazing. That was really thoughtful of you. That money is going to help the YWCA do a lot of good. Frankly, I'm impressed, Mr. Jackson."

"Well, thank you. I've been kicking some ideas around. You know, Caroline gets a lot of requests from nonprofits for appearances or money or endorsements, whatever. I'm going to start giving back more. It was recently brought to my attention that I can be pretty selfish." He gave her a boyish grin.

"Well I'm glad to see that you're changing your ways," Katie teased. She didn't resist when he leaned down to press his lips against hers. His warm kiss sent a shiver down her spine and reminded her why she fell for Blake in the first place.

"Is this okay?" he whispered against her lips. He closed his eyes and touched his forehead to hers.

"Yes," she whispered.

Blake took her hand and led Katie out of the room and into the empty hallway. "I have something for you." His eyes danced as he pulled a thick manila folder out of his jacket pocket and handed it to Katie. "Open it."

She pulled out a sheaf of papers and scanned the type, her brow furrowed in concentration. Blake watched her carefully, waiting for her reaction.

"You should go over it in detail later, before you sign it. I wanted to give it to you tonight to show you how serious I am about you and your career. It's a new contract, if you're interested. It's an offer to join me in a legal partnership. If you accept, then you will no longer be a hired musician for the band. You'll be my partner. It gives you more stability, more ownership and involvement in the music. What do you think?"

"Oh my gosh, this is amazing. This is huge. I don't know what to say." Katie's hand trembled as she tried to focus enough to read the words on the pages, unshed tears blurring her vision.

"You don't have to say anything. I want you to know that, without any doubt, I want you here with me for the long haul and I think we'll make a great team. This is not a favor or a gift. It's going to be a lot of hard work, but it's a solid career move for you, if you decide to take the next step. I want to make it clear to you that you will not be my employee, we will be partners in this."

"I am overwhelmed. I honestly never expected anything like this."

"I hope this will show you how serious I am about you, as a musician and as my partner." He cupped her face in his hands and looked into her eyes. "I swear to you, Katie McCoy, that I will never hurt you again. I will spend the rest of my life showing you how much you mean to me." He kissed her full on the lips and whispered, "If you'll let me."

He wrapped his arms around her, and she inhaled deeply, breathing in the scent that she had missed so much when they were apart. She felt his comforting warmth envelope her and could feel his heart beating next to hers. When Blake held her in his arms, Katie felt like she had come home. She had found her perfect fit, and she never wanted to let go.

She lifted her face and looked into his eyes, those blue eyes that told her he meant every word he said. She looked into the face that she loved so much, and words failed her. She pulled him down to meet her and kissed him. As he deepened the kiss, she could taste his minty toothpaste and found herself intoxicated by the spicy scent of his cologne, the warmth of his familiar body pressed against hers. It was everything that she had missed when they were apart. Her head was spinning and her toes were tingling. Her mind couldn't focus on anything except the delicious sensations swirling through her. How could she not take him back? This is where she belonged, in his arms and at his side.

Chapter Sixteen

Katie woke up in her Denver, Colorado hotel room on the morning of her twenty-fifth birthday and stretched, enjoying the deliciously soft hotel sheets. The room was beautifully appointed, one of the best money could buy, but the silence, the beautiful golden silence, was the most decadent luxury. The tour had landed in Denver early the morning before and the band had been given a free day to refresh before the show tonight. True to his word, Blake had used his time between the Wichita show and the band's stop in Denver, Colorado to respond to charity requests and schedule appearances that he would have skipped in the past. Yesterday he had installed Katie in the luxurious hotel room and left her in the capable hands of the staff massage therapist and aesthetician. She had spent the day getting kneaded and scrubbed while Blake had made an appearance at a local children's charity event. The day of pampering and the fancy hotel room had been an early birthday gift from Blake, and if she were to be honest, it was sorely needed.

The new touring and practice schedule had taken its toll on Katie and it was beginning to show in the dark circles that had taken up residence under her eyes. She had worked hard in Sterling, but life on tour with a major national act was like nothing she'd ever experienced before.

This morning, though, well-rested and completely refreshed, Katie was ready to get back to work. She called for room service to deliver breakfast and started her shower. The luxurious appointments reminded her how lucky she was. It was only because of Blake that she was even in Denver, much less spending her morning surrounded by luxury. He was shaping up to be a pretty good boyfriend. Working on her birthday would actually be a treat this year, and it was Blake who had made her dream job a reality. She massaged shampoo and conditioner through her hair and let her mind drift to the kiss she and Blake had shared in Wichita after he had given her the partnership papers.

Perhaps it had been too easy for her to slip back into his arms, but she was tired of resisting him, of denying herself what she wanted, what she needed. He was making changes in himself and the partnership agreement proved to her that he was serious. Katie wanted to believe that Blake had been as miserable as she had been when they were apart, that he would never let her go again. She had signed the contracts and was optimistic about their future together both professionally and romantically. For now, Blake was her everything, and the thought of losing him again felt like losing part of herself.

Katie wrapped herself in the hotel's plush robe and lounged on the bed while she waited for breakfast to arrive. She pulled her fingers through the tangles in her wet hair and wished that she had ordered coffee with breakfast. There was a knock at the door and she pulled her robe tighter, checking to be sure that she was completely covered up. She was surprised to see Blake instead of the room service attendant when she got to the door.

"Happy Birthday, sweetheart," he said with a grin before leaning in for a sweet kiss. He held up a package adorned with a giant fluffy pink bow.

Katie stepped aside as Blake entered the room. She couldn't keep the smile from her face. "I thought you would be room service."

"Sorry, no pancakes here, but I did bring you something."

Blake led her to the bed and sat her down before placing the package beside her. He grinned like a school boy and sat down beside her. "Open it."

Katie pulled the ribbon to unfasten the bow and tore the paper off the package. "You didn't have to do this. You've already done so much for me." She lifted the lid off the box and gasped as tears filled her eyes. She covered her mouth with her hands and looked up at Blake. "Oh my gosh, it's gorgeous! Thank you!" Her tears began flowing in earnest as she took in the gift and the look of adoration in Blake's eyes.

"I'm glad you like it. Happy birthday, sweetheart."

Blake had given Katie a gorgeous new fiddle, one that was nicer than she had ever played and certainly nicer than the battered instrument she had been dragging across the country. Her old fiddle had seen her through good times and bad and she would always love it, but the new one was amazing. And it was from Blake, given to her on her twenty-fifth birthday, and every time she looked at it, she would remember this day.

"I know that musicians can get attached to their instruments, so I promise you it won't hurt my feelings if you still use the old one. Absolutely no pressure."

"Oh my gosh, no! I'm going to start using this one tonight if I can. It's amazing. This might be the nicest gift anyone has ever given me." Tears threatened to fill her eyes again, but her breakfast finally did arrive and she allowed the room service attendant to distract her.

He grinned at her and got to his feet. "Have your breakfast, sweetheart, and get yourself ready for the day. I've got more surprises for the birthday girl later. I'm afraid if I stay in here with you in nothing but that robe for much longer I'll miss my afternoon appointments." Blake winked and pulled Katie into his arms and held her close. "Take your time getting ready and I'll see you in a bit." He looked down at her and smoothed a wet lock of hair behind her ear before pressing a soft kiss on her lips. He raked his eyes over her, bit his lip, and let out a low whistle before stepping back with obvious effort and leaving her alone in the hotel room.

• • •

The stage lights were blazing and the floor rumbled beneath her feet, shaking from the noise of the crowd. Katie looked at the set list taped to the back of her monitor and saw "KATIE" scrawled in black marker between the neatly written song names of the familiar show order.

She looked across the stage to find Blake already watching her, his expression mischievous. He pulled an acoustic guitar onto his lap as he perched on a stool in the middle of the stage. The other musicians set their instruments on racks and moved to the side of the stage to watch, apparently already aware of what was going on.

Blake winked at Katie and pulled the microphone down to meet his lips. "Hello, Denver!" The crowd screamed and flashes went off as people took pictures. "Tonight is a special night, and I'm so happy that you're here for it. We're celebrating a very special birthday." He held his hand out and gestured towards Katie, who was frozen in place. "Happy Birthday, baby." He absentmindedly picked out the notes to 'Happy Birthday' on his guitar as he looked out into the audience with a wide smile.

The audience roared, and Katie felt her face flush as she realized that all attention was on her. She put her fiddle on its stand and turned towards Blake, clasping her hands at her heart as tears welled in her eyes.

"Have you ever met someone who seemed like they were made just for you? Someone so special that it was almost too good to be true? I have. I've also screwed the whole thing up. I had the perfect woman right in front of me, and I let her go. We don't always get a second chance, but this time I did. I'll never make the same mistake again."

Blake turned to Katie and mouthed the words, "I love you." Katie's heart squeezed and buttery warmth spread through her, all the way down to her toes.

He pulled the strap of his acoustic guitar over his shoulder and settled himself on the wooden stool before adjusting the microphone. "I wrote a little song for the lovely, talented, incomparable Katie McCoy, and I hope you'll indulge me while I share it with y'all." The crowd shouted their approval, and Blake strummed a couple of chords on his guitar before clearing his throat. He gave the crowd a toothy smile and said, "Thanks y'all. You're the first people I've ever played it for, so here goes."

"From the moment that I saw you, all I wanted was to kiss you. I knew that if you left me, all I could do would be to miss you. Kiss me, Katie, if you love me like I love you. Kiss me, Katie. I've had days and weeks when I've thought of only you. I'll die a happy man if you love me like I love you. I dream of your eyes, your lips, your sweet smile. I've had days when being a foot away from you felt like a mile. Kiss me, Katie, if you love me like I love you. Kiss me, Katie."

Katie willed herself to focus on the words of Blake's song and forced herself to hold back the tears that were threatening to spill over onto her beautifully applied makeup. On shaking legs, she found herself propelled across the stage towards Blake without ever consciously deciding to go to him. The magnetic attraction she had always felt for him was pulling her closer to him, drawing her to his side.

His voice filled her head and everything else fell away. There were only the two of them, no hot stage lights, no screaming crowd, no band members at the edge of the stage. She reached Blake and took his face in her hands, dimly aware that he had stopped singing, and kissed him full on the lips. Reality came crashing back as he returned the kiss and the crowd erupted into ear-splitting cheers. She pulled back a bit, suddenly aware that she had kissed Blake Jackson in front of several thousand strangers, and bit her lip. He pulled her back towards him, until their foreheads touched, and looked into her eyes. Katie was pressed awkwardly against Blake's guitar, but his strong arm around her waist and his warm hand holding her close felt so right that she didn't want to move.

"I love you, and I always will." Blake's voice was husky. He pressed another sweet kiss on her lips, and Katie threw her arms around his shoulders and squeezed. She felt the love in his kiss, but finally hearing the words was pure magic.

"I love you, too. I always will." Katie couldn't keep the smile off her face as she pulled herself away from Blake and forced herself to walk back to her spot on the stage. From now on, her place was by Blake's side, and she had come home. She picked up her fiddle as the rest of the band returned to the stage, grinning at her and Blake and shaking their heads. They had never seen him like this. Blake blew her a kiss, handed his acoustic guitar to a roadie, and held his arms out to the crowd.

"Sorry about that, guess I just couldn't resist. Look at her, though, I mean, who can blame me? Now, I suppose you good people want to hear more of what you came here for. One, two, three, four!" He counted off and the band started their next song.

A Sneak Peek from Crimson Romance

(From *Nightingale* by Sharon Ervin)

Great Britain, 1840

The earth trembled and Jessica Blair's bare feet flew over the narrow dirt path, which was still warm at twilight after the first sunny day of spring. The rumbling was too steady to herald artillery or a turn in the weather. It was hooves and they sounded as if the horses were closing rapidly.

Jessica hiked up her skirt, wadded it over an arm and broke into a full, unladylike gallop. She hadn't taken time to put on the oversized lace-up boots, which jostled clumsily under one elbow. Her lungs burned as she pushed her lean young body, desperate to reach the coops and protect the newly emerged chicks. Their lives depended on her. She had vowed to protect and defend them from all enemies, foreign or domestic. Giving her oath before the nine scruffy hens, Jessica had contemplated enemies like foxes or raccoons. Nevertheless, she would defend them, her body of no more value to the world than theirs, if measured by the meager living she eked out for herself and her ailing, widowed mother.

The thunderous pounding grew louder. Foliage snapped and lowering tree limbs cracked as the relentless riders plundered the path behind her. Jessica needed to reach the twin boulders. She had chosen the site for her coops, thinking the promontories would protect the rickety pens. The stone outcroppings loomed side by side, separated only by the width of her narrow shoulders.

In her weeks of coming and going, Jessica inadvertently had worn a path to the place, one clearly visible even in the fading daylight. Her frequent use had widened it; perhaps giving the impression the path was a thoroughfare. It was not.

Jessica sliced between the twins and burst into the clearing. Dropping her boots and wadded skirts, she doubled over, bracing her hands on her knees, gulping air to feed her burning lungs. Her abrupt arrival set the roosting hens squawking in alarm, batting about in the cages she had constructed from scraps of barrels, and hoops from discarded casks.

In spite of her heart's pounding, she heard the relentless thud of hooves, clanging metal and fierce snorting as if the hounds of hell pursued the horses.

Straightening, suddenly aware of the coming darkness, she realized riders galloping headlong over the trail she had cut, probably would not see the stone pillars until they were upon them. She cringed at the image of animals and men injured or killed in the collision, harsh punishment for following her unwitting footpath.

Her breathing steadied, she slid back between the twins and studied the approach with no clear plan, only the hope she could stop the riders before their flight ended in disaster.

A horse exploded out of the night, hurtling toward her, a huge, black beast, his rounded eyes glistening, steam hissing from red, flaring nostrils. She flailed her arms and yelled. "Halt!"

The rider did not slow. He must be a stupid oaf to propel himself and his mount over such a poorly marked course. Still, she did not want the man to die of his stupidity and certainly could not allow such a ghastly end to his horse.

Fanning her skirts to gain attention, she screamed, "Halt! In the name of the Queen!" It was the only command she thought might bring the intemperate soul to his senses. She braced, prepared to jump to either side to avoid being trampled.

The first horse was almost on top of her when he suddenly planted his front feet, sat back on his haunches and skidded. Just before impact, he reared straight up. His hooves fanned the air over her head. Jessica threw her arms up as a shield and leaped to her left, squeezing her eyes closed.

An instant later, when there was no contact, she opened one eye to find the horse's front hooves still high above her head, striking one another and producing sparks which resembled a bevy of fireflies.

"Whoa," she shouted.

With snorting that sounded like a groan, the animal dropped his forefeet to the ground. His massive body quivered as he danced sideways. His eyes rolled and his sides heaved as horse and woman stood facing one another.

In her eighteen years, Jessica had never been that close to a horse and this one seemed particularly large and noisy, snorting and wheezing in turn.

"There, there, love," she crooned, certain she was more frightened than the animal. "It is only I, Sweetness, Jessica Blair." She resisted the impulse to look anywhere but into the horse's bulbous eyes. "Welcome to you and your intemperate master to my humble hatches." She smirked at the purposeful insult directed at the unseen rider.

When the rider didn't respond, she glanced up and leaned around only to find the saddle empty.

The destrier threw his head high and pranced in place. Metal clanked against metal, the noise she had identified before she had been able to see him.

"Where is your master, love?" She regarded him closely. "Is he lying in the road somewhere injured? He's not dead, is he, Sweetness?"

Eying her wildly, the horse lifted his nose then lowered it in a series of nods.

Jessica swallowed and eased closer. Raising an uncertain hand, she started to touch him, and then stopped. She wanted to quiet the magnificent animal, and he did seem to be calming.

"My, but you are huge," she whispered. His restless movements stopped and his ears flicked forward. "Your color is like midnight and you have a look of enchantment, all spirit and size and muscle." She lifted a hand again to touch him. He threw his head high and she gasped to see his neck slathered with thick white foam.

"What is this?" She studied the goo spattered over his chest and stringing from the dangling strap. She wiped a glob off him and cringed as it clung to her curious fingers. "Are you injured?"

The horse tossed his head, keeping his nose well above her reach while his occasional snorts dwindled to a nervous whickering. She flinched when he lowered his nose and bumped the side of her face. "Even if he mistreated you, you would not have thrown the dullard for revenge, would you? Of course you didn't. It is the role of some to serve and of others to be served. Like me, you appear to be the former."

She fingered the horse's bridle trying to think what she should do. He danced back several steps, his agitation reviving, reminding her that her voice quieted him.

"I have never had a private conversation with a horse." Again, her words calmed him. At her quiet stroking, her fingertips on his face, the animal eased closer. Prickling chills limned her arms as the horse nuzzled her hair, his breath warm against her sensitive nape. When he nibbled a strand of hair, she jerked, startling them both.

"Mind your manners, sir."

As if he understood, he steadied, his neck arched, his feet still. He glistened black beneath the globs of white froth that oozed and abandoned him in dollops. His saddle and tack were black to match his body. No wonder she hadn't been able to see him in the twilight or that one horse his size could sound like many.

She knew no better than to walk behind his rump, but he stood unmoving as her hands ran over his sides, swiping away the last remnants of the froth.

His master must be a large man, judging by the size of this animal and the length of the stirrups. An average-sized individual could scarcely throw a leg over such a monster.

Wondering again what had become of the rider; she turned and peered into the night, straining to see if a form lay on the footpath. She had neither seen nor heard anyone in the darkness, which had completely enveloped them. A full moon slipped for a moment from beneath its cloudy sheath to bathe the open area where they stood. The path beyond, however, was cloaked in the shadowy gloom of overhanging trees.

The horse had galloped, wild-eyed, snorting and whinnying as if the devil himself were in pursuit. Had his master mistreated him?

No. She had felt no welts of scarring. No blemishes of any kind. The clattering his hooves created earlier indicated he was shod. He appeared well fed and his coat was sleek, as if it were brushed regularly.

Perhaps his master had overindulged at a tavern and fallen off. Perhaps the man had been set upon by a thief. She considered again the length of the stirrups. It would probably have taken more than one thief to subdue this rider.

Perhaps she should search for him. How could she? A lone woman? Traveling the road at night? Especially if there were brigands about. She had nothing to steal, of course. She slanted her gaze at the horse. Except him. She would need to take him along in case they found his rider, particularly if they found the man incapacitated.

She stood on tiptoe to work the rein off over the horse's ears, then she looped the leather around a branch and ran back to the coops for her boots. As she put them on, she considered. In the dark, she might overlook a man lying in the brush at the side of the road. It would be wiser to wait for daylight.

She cast a guilty glance at the moon that beamed at the moment, denying her use of darkness as an excuse not to try.

If the man were lying in the road, some passerby probably already had rescued him.

What if he lay helpless? Or unconscious? Or dead?

Her imagination erupted with visions of a helpless wretch lying injured, crying out for assistance while help was delayed, wrestling with her own cowardice.

She resented the nudge, the same goading presence that prompted her to rescue abandoned birds and runaway horses. Could she, in good conscience, comfort the man's animal and not expend some effort searching for the master?

If she could ride the horse, the search would be easier. Also, mounted, she would feel less vulnerable to attack by men or animals.

She had never ridden a horse.

The decision would rest with him. If Sweetness would let her climb into the saddle, she would track back along the road, at least a little distance.

Returning to the horse, Jessica freed the rein and slipped her hand beneath the strap between his ear and his mouth. She applied pressure and he rocked into step beside her. She led him in a wide circle to line him up beside a fallen log, and again fitted the rein over his head.

How should she sit? The saddle was not properly cut for her to ride with her legs to one side, as ladies of the gentry rode. Her oversized dress and petticoat, a cousin's castoffs, might be generous enough to allow her to ride astride as a man would.

Speaking those thoughts quietly to the horse, Jessica stepped onto the log.

As large as it was, the saddle would provide ample seating. She fingered the leather strap, stalling. Brushing a hand over the saddle, front to back, she slipped a knot and accidentally released a garment tied behind.

The horse held steady as Jessica unfurled the rolled fabric. When she snapped the garment open, the mount's eyes rolled, but he only turned his head, as if curious to see what she was doing. It was a cloak, black of course, like the horse and his other accessories. It smelled of wool mingled with a distinctly male fragrance that was not altogether unpleasant. The weave was as soft as Mrs. Maxwell's silken stockings.

"This will serve," she whispered. If she could get into the saddle, she could wrap the cloak around her, and conceal her long, dark hair beneath the hood. Travelers would think her a young man. A youth traveling alone at night would be less remarkable than a girl. Hopefully no one would consider accosting him.

First, however, she must get herself into the saddle.

Would the owner of the horse be angry when she appeared in his clothing riding his horse? Would he accuse her of theft?

Perhaps not, if she rescued him. She prayed to find him in desperate need of saving. Incapacitated, maybe. Not dead.

"Oh, Lord, please don't let him be dead."

What would she do if she found him dead?

She would turn the horse around and return to the coops to devise another plan. Now, however, she needed to concentrate on mounting this enormous beast.

Bracing her feet on the fallen log, Jessica raised her skirts to her knees. She took great handfuls of the mane low on his neck, stretched onto her toes, kicked her right leg up and partially over the saddle.

The horse nickered, but did not move. Jessica teetered, her legs spread in a ridiculous, untenable position. Bouncing on the lower foot, she thrust herself up. Straining, pulling, levering her right leg over the saddle, she kicked, lifted and tugged. With one heave, she acquired the seat, and a split second later clawed frantically to keep from hurtling headfirst off the other side.

In another moment, she sat quaking, surprised and pleased to be securely seated, and drew a shuddering breath.

Sitting a horse so far above the ground was at once terrifying and exhilarating. Brazenly she perched there, her skirt wadded high on her thighs, her lone petticoat scarcely covering her knees, and her legs cradling the massive animal. Her mother's words echoed in her head. "A proper lady keeps her knees together."

But her widowed mother was some distance away and that advice, sage as it might normally be, did not anticipate the current situation. Her mother also had bid Jessica to use her own good judgment, not to be swayed from a proper course by circumstances or the opinions or behavior of others, which was, of course, precisely what she was doing.

Squirming, Jessica tugged at her skirt, modesty requiring that she cover as much of her limbs as possible. In the process, she stretched her legs, which were long for a woman, and the reason for most of her height, but, even pointing her toes, she was not able to reach the stirrups.

"All right," she said, addressing the stirrups, "we shall manage quite nicely without you." She smirked at her use of the royal we.

Shivering with dread or excitement, Jessica arranged the heavy cloak around her shoulders and took comfort in the protection even as it swallowed her. Then she raised the rein high, as she had seen men driving plow horses do, giving what she hoped was the signal to go.

Nothing happened.

"All right," she said and bounced a little in her seat. "Go!"

Nothing.

She leaned to put her mouth as close to the horse's ear as possible. "It must be obvious, Sweetness, I have no idea what I am about. Be merciful. Take me by the swiftest path straight to your master." As she straightened from the tête-à-tête, her heels slid along the horse's flanks.

As if he had understood her words, Sweetness moved several paces forward. Jessica rewarded his effort with high praise and series of staccato pats on the neck. As she straightened, her heels again grazed the horse's sides and again he advanced.

"That's good. That is very good indeed." In her enthusiasm, she pulled back on the rein. He stopped.

Experimentally, she rubbed her heels lightly at his flanks. The horse advanced, slowly at first until Jessica adapted to his gait. Gradually he accelerated until, with no leave from his rider, he lengthened his stride to a gentle lope as they emerged from the path onto the commercial roadway. Feeling at one with the horse, her body rocking in sync with his, Jessica smiled, then laughed out loud at her success.

Clutching the rein, she pulled the cloak more tightly about her and felt as if she had died and gone to heaven. Denied the use of the stirrups, she gripped with her feet, cradling the horse's barreled body until her legs quivered with the strain.

The animal moved effortlessly, requiring no guidance, back the way he had come. He seemed to know where they were going. As the distance grew, Jessica began to note landmarks to assist in her eventual return, a trip she anticipated she would make on foot.

The horse's easy lope became a canter as the distance between Jessica and her coops lengthened and the night deepened.

At first she welcomed the bite of the determined little breeze in her face, but after a while it became worrisome and she drew the cloak's hood over her head and down to cover her eyes and nose. She had little need to see since her companion obviously had their destination in mind.

They traveled for what seemed like an hour as the breeze became wind. Clouds, in turn, played hide and seek with the lemony moon.

Her mother would assume the scullery maids had drawn additional duties at the manor house. Also, her mother knew Jessica's lack of interest in keeping to schedules.

Still, she was her mother's last child, subject to the overprotection of that position. She did not trouble her ailing parent without good cause. A man lost, perhaps dying on the road, qualified. But how far had they come? How much farther must they go to find him?

As the wind slapped tree branches overhead, Jessica wrapped the cloak more tightly and found comfort in the musky fragrance of the garment.

There were few travelers on the road, a half-dozen were afoot and not inclined to look up, or address a dark rider as they passed. Other riders were more interested in Sweetness than in the shadowy form in his saddle.

After her initial excitement, the perpetual rhythm of the horse's hooves, her long day of work in the manor house and her wild flight through the woods took their toll. Jessica nodded only to jerk awake when Sweetness slowed his pace, accommodating her each time the rein slipped from her hands or she slid one way or the other in the saddle.

She roused wide-eyed, however, when her mount began high-stepping and sidling. Perhaps they were nearing his home. She had heard that horses often raced out of control when they neared their barns; therefore, she was puzzled when the huge animal slowed instead of charging ahead. He stopped altogether and turned a wide circle in the road.

Fully awake, Jessica gently applied her heels to his sides. He refused to go.

Without a step to aid her dismount, Jessica gripped the front and rear of the saddle, braced her weight on her hands, worked her legs to the same side of the horse, and then let herself drop.

When her feet met the earth, she stumbled and grabbed a stirrup bar to keep herself upright.

Scoring the more-or-less successful dismount as another accomplishment, she looked at the horse, expecting guidance. His eyes rolled as he tossed his head and nickered, dancing sideways, but moving neither forward nor back.

She pulled the rein over his ears and down to lead him, but when she attempted to advance the direction they had been traveling, he balked.

She regarded him with some annoyance as he jerked his nose skyward and blew a loud whinny into the night.

"What is it?" she asked.

The horse bobbed his head up and down, making the hardware on his bridle jangle loudly in the eerie silence.

Cajoling, coaxing, Jessica turned him around and attempted to walk back the way they had come. Again Sweetness set his feet and refused.

Was he daft? She had come this far. She had no intention of simply abandoning this magnificent creature on a commercial road at night.

Tossing his head, he whinnied and pawed the ground.

Trees and brambles lined both sides of the road. Jessica shivered, feeling an ominous presence. Traveling any direction would be safer than standing in the middle of this deserted highway.

The huge horse shook his head and tamped the soft ground.

Jessica stroked his nose. "Come, Sweetness. Please. We need to be away from this place."

Wind rustling nearby trees produced noises that sounded like human groans. Fearful yet curious, Jessica couldn't help peering into the shadows beneath the swaying branches.

"All right," she said, keeping her voice low to mask the panic inside. She swept off the cloak and anchored it behind the saddle, then sucked up her courage and stepped off the road to their left, the direction Sweetness indicated, squirreling in among the trees, tugging the now-docile animal along behind her.

Metal pieces on the horse's bridle jingled as he followed, as obedient as a lamb. She found the familiar sound reassuring. She led him on, adjusting their course toward the moans that came more frequently and more audibly as she and the jingling, willing mount moved deeper into the wood.

The moans could be coming from an injured animal—a wolf or boar or even a bear recently roused from a winter's sleep and hungry. Surely Sweetness would not follow if he sensed a predator. Of course, he was the same animal who had raced headlong down a footpath and might have broken his neck on the boulders if she had not waved him off. She probably shouldn't rely too heavily on his judgment.

Several yards into the underbrush, Jessica came to a barrier of thistled shrubs. The peculiar moaning sounded as if it were just beyond.

Releasing the horse, Jessica dropped onto her hands and knees to push through the prickly undergrowth. Thorns snagged her shoulders and knifed through worn sleeves to puncture her flesh. She bit her lips to keep from crying out, yielding only an occasional whimper that mingled melodiously with the night birds cooing on their roosts, warbling to report her passing.

Wriggling, she burrowed on, listening for the human sound, tuning out the birds' night calls. Pausing, holding her breath for silence, she heard the distinct sound of running water.

It was neither sight nor hearing, finally, but Jessica's sense of smell that urged her forward. The familiar fragrance of the cloak drew her—a scent which had been both shield and ally during the long uncertain moments of her ride—into a small clearing.

In the dappled lighting beneath a willow, lay a bundle roughly the size and shape of a man's head. She scrabbled closer, settling a foot away from the bundle.

"Hello." She nudged the mound with two fingers. "Please tell me you are a human being and that you are alive."

No response.

Her breath caught as she considered, then reworded her plea. "Please, please do not be a man dead."

A groan prefaced movement. One booted foot rustled leaves six feet away as a ruddy face framed by a mop of pale, tousled hair, floated up from the debris at her fingertips. She scrabbled back.

His flesh looked mottled in the intermittent moonlight through the trees. The face mumbled a string of what might have been coarse language, before the man hiked himself onto an elbow. His eyes were open, but didn't appear to focus. His voice emerged as a snarl.

"I can scarcely move my legs, my head is pounding, and my throat is on fire." He paused. "Alive or dead? You pronounce."

Jessica allowed a smile. If he were able to speak so of his situation, he must be better off than he sounded…or looked.

Her questions came rapid-fire. "What happened? Who are you? What would you have me do?"

His eyes rolled and he blinked but appeared confused. The spotty moonlight sporadically peeped from the branches overhead. Clouds swept the restless nighttime sky. A smudge on the man's forehead ebbed and flowed in the shadows. The blemish might be blood seeping from a wound.

Another shadow, one she decided was facial hair, circled his mouth and made him appear at once sinister and provocative. A thin beard followed the line of his jaws from the goatee to sideburns in the fashion of the day. The man looked to be of unusual size, well conformed, and perhaps even comely.

Spurred by the ooze that trickled into his brow, Jessica leaped up, again aware of the sound of running water.

"I'll be right back."

The man flapped his free hand wildly at the emptiness between them, wheezing objections as she rustled beyond his reach.

Ducking, she wriggled through another span of undergrowth, gained her feet and found a brook not fifty feet from the man's position.

The hem of her worn petticoat tore easily. She rinsed and wrung the scrap, let it soak, then squeezed it only a little as she regained her feet and scurried back to the man.

On her knees at his side, she pressed the dripping cloth to his lips. He clamped a huge hand onto her wrist as he sucked enough water from the rag to swallow twice before he spoke.

"Are you an angel?" The words were soft, but his voice sounded stronger. "Your song is a solo in the forest's chorale." He attempted a smile. "It trills, like a nightingale." He sniffed the air. "Your fragrance, too, is cleansing." He frowned. "Are you real?"

She smiled and wiped the cloth gently over his features, working around the beard, cleaning smudges that could be removed from his face. Other shadowy presences appeared to be bruises.

"No, I am not an angel, and this nest where you roost might be fit for a nightingale, but it is not Heaven."

His features relaxed. "Good. The discomfort here is more than I expected of Heaven." He arched an eyebrow. "Not as severe as I imagined Hell."

She rewarded his jocular effort with a little laugh, but continued her ministrations.

As she brushed leaves aside and his person came into full view, Jessica was impressed by the man's size. Nicely made, he had breadth to match his length, which spanned six feet or more from his head to his toes.

"What happened?" she asked, dusting debris from his shoulders.

"I objected to being robbed. I put a ball through one and my blade through another before someone bashed me in the head. My last clear memory is of pulling my feet out of the stirrups. I did not want death to catch me beneath the heels of my temperamental steed. The lack wits beat me some, but it was a halfhearted effort."

"Thank a merciful God for that."

He cleared his throat. "Of course." His eyes didn't follow as she crawled around him, raking away leaves and twigs. Instead, he gazed blankly into the emptiness where she had been. Interrupting her raking, Jessica again used the dampened rag to mop bits of blood from the man's neck. The sticky liquid had saturated his neck cloth. Her touch startled him and he looked momentarily alarmed before he checked that reaction in favor of another.

"Thank you," he said, turning his head in what appeared an attempt to address her face. "Vindicator is an exemplary war horse, but not at all adept as a nursemaid."

The man groaned as he pushed all the way to a sitting position. His supporting arm trembled and Jessica pushed her shoulder closer to steady him and, perhaps, conserve what remained of his strength.

"Later, I roused," he continued, as if eager to recall the happenings for his own hearing. "Men argued. It was full dark by then, the night like pitch, as it is now." He rolled his eyes and waited, apparently giving her time to confirm or refute the darkness.

She glanced at the moon. For the moment, it illuminated their surroundings and gave form to shapes around them.

She didn't speak, instead resumed her work with the cloth. She dabbed a splotch from his full lower lip. My, he seemed a handsome man. His eyes were deep set but squinting, perhaps against the headache he mentioned. The trim beard gave him a look of devil-may-care abandon and, at the same time, of authority.

Her swabbing reopened a wound at his hairline freeing blood to trickle anew down his forehead.

"I crawled into the weeds, thinking to hide until my sight cleared," he said, seemingly oblivious to her ongoing ministrations.

"I wanted my head to stop pounding and the world to cease spinning. I made for the sound of water. I didn't get there, did I?"

"You are very close," she said. Jessica was wiping scratches and scrapes on his hands, but neither those minor abrasions nor the cuts on his forehead were severe enough to be the source of the gummy dampness soaking his shirt collar and neck cloth.

Carefully, she brushed her hands over his face, which he moved with her touch. Her fingers rasped over the narrow beard as she ran them into the thick hair above his ears, searching for the source of the profuse bleeding that had begun again in earnest.

Suddenly her roving fingers slid into a warm moist well and the man shouted a barrage of what sounded like fluent French profanity.

"Be still." Her voice rang with a competence she did not feel.

Changing position, scooting on her knees to get closer, Jessica steeled herself as her fingers cautiously tracked the blood back to a long, deep gash at the base of his skull. She traced the cut, trying to determine its length and depth.

"Have care!" He snapped the words, but remained still as she continued her probe, attempting to see with fingertips that came away dripping blood.

She shook out an unused strip of the dampened petticoat and dabbed at the gouge. When that scrap was soaked and unmanageably sticky, she tore a dry length from the garment.

"Be still," she repeated, again assuming the authority of the one in charge while attempting to hide her own uncertainty.

He stiffened, started to speak, then, apparently reconsidered, and did as he was told. Perhaps he was a soldier, accustomed to taking orders. No, he wore fine clothes and the boots of a gentleman, not a uniform.

She wrapped the new length of cloth twice around his head and tucked the loose end into itself before checking the improvised bandage. The covering crossed one of his eyes then circled his crown giving him the look of a buccaneer. Jessica disregarded his evil appearance, satisfied that the wrapping covered the wound. She had secured it tightly enough to reduce the free flow of blood to an ooze.

Jessica crawled all the way around him, surveying, but found no other gashes, although shadows played tricks, occasionally making it appear there were more splotches, each of which she investigated despite the man's grating objections. The wound on the back of his head looked to be the worst of it.

As she examined him, she attempted to revive their earlier conversation. "Has your head stopped pounding and spinning now?"

He squinted and cautiously tilted his head. "Not yet. Tell me, child, how did you come to be here in the dark? It is not yet morning, is it? We are still well hidden, are we not?"

Just as she had guessed, in spite of his denials, he realized the problem with his eyesight involved more than poor lighting. She would play along, not dispute his references to the darkness.

"Sweetness. Your horse brought me."

"Not my horse. My horse's name is Vindicator."

"I see."

"Are you part of a search party sent from Gull's Way?"

"No, sir. I came alone."

Her statement seemed to annoy him. "What do you mean?"

"I rode Sweet…the horse, sir."

"My mount's name is Vindicator. He comes from a long line of warhorses revered for their courage in battle. He is not fit for a woman to ride. It was not Vindicator who brought you here." He sounded insufferably, unyieldingly certain.

She frowned into the pale face as he sat cross-legged, staring at nothing. His one uncovered eye shifted anxiously. Obviously he could not see and felt threatened by her nearness.

"I see no reason to argue, sir, over your mount's name or lineage." She liked sounding so mature and reasonable. "A large, gentle, black horse carried me to this place and…"

"Are you an experienced rider?"

"No."

"Well then, it's exactly as I said. The animal that brought you here is not Vindicator. He has thrown every man who has attempted to ride him, including me, until we reached an understanding. In seven years in my stables, Vindicator has accepted no other rider. I personally bred his dam to the finest stallion in all of Britain. Vindicator's bloodlines rival those of the nation's finest families."

Jessica fought her vexation at this injured man who insisted on pursuing an inane argument about a horse.

"Please, sir, might we discuss your horse's name, his ancestry, or his philosophy of life another time? We have more pressing concerns."

His lips twitched and she thought he almost smiled, and then appeared to catch himself. "I am merely assuring you that the animal you rode to my rescue here tonight is not my horse." The man suddenly puckered his lips and gave a sharp, clear whistle.

Beyond the foliage, the horse whickered.

The man scowled, bleated a dismissive, "Ahh," and set his sightless eye back on his companion. "What is your name, child?"

She stumbled getting to her feet, but answered curtly. "My name is Jessica Blair, sir, and I am a woman grown, not a child."

Eying him, she puzzled as another smile nearly escaped his constraint. She had real difficulties to overcome at the moment without wasting precious time speculating about this stranger's mercurial smile.

Jessica stepped to her right just as a breeze sorted nearby leaves, masking the sound of her movement. The man's face did not follow. As he continued looking sternly at the place she had been, he lowered his voice to a coaxing tone.

"You sound like an intelligent girl, Jessica Blair. Have you not learned that lies seldom improve one's position?"

He tried to stand, but as he did so, his poor, injured head grazed a low limb. He flinched and bent, looking uncertain and thoroughly vulnerable.

Jessica wanted to be as truthful as possible with this man whom she now felt certain had no sight at all. "I lie, sir, only when I deem it entirely necessary."

Still stooped, he turned abruptly, addressing the place where her words originated. "And stop calling me 'sir.'" He hesitated, then lowered his voice to a kinder tone. "I am properly addressed as 'Your Grace.'"

Again he tried to straighten, presumably to assume the regal stance of someone of importance, and again banged his poor head into the same low-hanging bough.

"A duke? You, sir, are a nobleman?" She took his hand and tugged him a step forward, out from under the abusive bough. As she did so, she tried to see beneath the dirt, the injuries, and his general dishabille. Except for the expensive clothes, he didn't look the part he claimed.

Still, she saw no benefit in arguing. "I fear the blow to your head did more damage than shows, Your Grace," she muttered. He had nerve, chastising her for suspected lies, then feigning lofty position.

The leaves whirled again and he started, obviously uneasy. She hurried her next words to placate him.

"Sweetness—that is, your horse—is strong, Your Grace, and uninjured. He doesn't even seem tired. You, on the other hand, are spent. We will get you mounted and deliver you to an inn. Surely there is one nearby where we can summon a physician."

"No." Fumbling, he flung a hand forward to brush then catch her wrist in a grip so firm she gasped. "You will convey me to my home."

"Tonight?"

He relaxed his grip slightly but maintained his hold on her arm. "Yes. At once."

"But you need a doctor."

"No." His grip on her wrist tightened.

She forced herself to hold silent.

"You must take me to Shiller's Green. My home, Gull's Way, is near there. Do you know the place?"

"No, Your Grace. I live near Welter. This is my first journey beyond the river valley."

"What are you doing here now then, alone, and at night?"

"As I told you...Your Grace," she stammered again over the title, "your horse brought me."

"A horse, like a soldier, goes where he's commanded."

"Your horse does not, Your Grace, to your good fortune." She didn't like seeing this large commanding man at a disadvantage, stooped as if he were cowering in the shadows. "Do you plan for us to cower here among the thistles and weeds debating all night?"

He seemed caught off guard by her brash words, then covered his surprise with bluster. "Of course not. However, I do expect you to provide a believable explanation of your presence here before this night is over. You would do well to come up with a more convincing story."

With that, he turned abruptly, as if leading a charge. Jessica stood glowering at the back of this man who displayed such a vexing lack of regard or appreciation for her considerable effort and inconvenience on his behalf.

After moments of flailing and being slapped this way and that by wayward branches, he finally set a steadying hand on the trunk of a sapling and assumed a mostly upright position.

Again taking his measure, Jessica straightened to her full height. He definitely was of a size to fit the huge horse waiting beyond the briars. How in heaven's name could she manage him through the underbrush and see him onto his immense mount? As she delayed, the man cocked his head as if listening to her thoughts.

Profoundly aware he could not see her, she had a fleeting, unconscionable thought. She could abandon him. Could take his precious horse, for that matter. He could scarcely prevent it.

Where had such an outrageous idea come from? It was more like John Lout than Jessica Blair. It was this man's fault. He annoyed her almost beyond patience. Of course, she could never live with herself if she left him helpless, friendless. Friendless was probably this man's usual condition, and through no fault of hers. Surely he displayed a more civil attitude toward his peers than he showed those less fortunate who were foolish enough to render aid.

As to his horse, the animal probably would refuse to go in any direction without him.

All right. She would see the ingrate to his horse and mounted. Then the four-legged one, which still had its eyesight and what appeared to be an unerring sense of direction, could deliver this duke home.

She regretted having told the man her name or having mentioned Welter. It would be better if she had simply reunited this insufferable soul with his steed then turned her feet toward home.

In the mood for more Crimson Romance?
Check out *Doubts of the Heart*
by Eva Shaw
at *CrimsonRomance.com*.

About the Author

Monica Tillery lives in Texas with her handsome husband of more than a dozen years, two sons, and a bunch of pets. Being the only girl in a house full of boys is so much fun, but her favorite things are romance novels, playing games with friends, girls' nights out, and her book club. Monica loves hearing from readers. Visit her at *www.monicatillery.com* to see all the ways to connect.